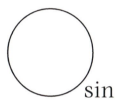

Osin

Jessica Lott

LOW FIDELITY PRESS

BIRMINGHAM, ALABAMA

Low Fidelity Press
1912 16th Avenue South
Birmingham, Alabama 35205-5607
info@lofipress.com
http://www.lofipress.com

Cover design: Andrew Vernon
Cover art: Graham Lott
Book design and typesetting: Ambivalent Design
Printed in the U.S.A. by United Graphics, Inc.

Library of Congress Cataloging-in-Publication Data
Lott, Jessica, 1974-
Osin / by Jessica Lott.
p. cm.
ISBN 0-9723363-7-0
1. Middle-aged men--Fiction. 2. Self-realization--Fiction. 3.
Marriage--Fiction. 4. Fatherhood--Fiction. I. Title.
PS3612.O777O85 2007
813'.6--dc22
2006103411

For my parents

I

It had been two weeks since Osin's wife Merrill had left him, and every afternoon around two he went looking for her. She had moved from their beautiful Marin home to an ugly, working class San Francisco suburb where children threw things at cars and the supermarkets were a low grade. He never ventured there. There was no need to; the probability was high that she was still shopping locally. Osin made a left and crept by the tinted windows of the Stop and Shop, watching the Mercedes's wavery and slightly menacing reflection.

Today he'd tried to repress the expedition by taking a nap, but he'd woken up while it was still light out. Only sixty-seven years old and he felt a hair's breadth from the big sleep every time he lay down. He now spent much of the day in bed. Before retiring from his publishing house last month, he bragged he would do nothing but read. He'd been the executive editor, and his staff had given him the complete set of Emerson's works as a goodbye gift, some of them rare editions. "For your new library" the card said. The box, unopened, sat at the base of the stairs.

Literature, that was a hobby. Amazing, really, the possibility that could be trapped between the covers of a book. His profession had been business books—how-to's—a lifetime spent convincing the average joe he could get himself rich for $24.95. He'd done a few titles for businessmen, but the biggest sellers always came with a video or a compact disc and were for the guy who understood money to be cash, not equity, who walked around like a kid with a dollar bill burning a hole through his pocket. It was the same principle as selling used cars, which he'd done as a teenager. A volume business. The real money was made off the trade-ins, off the guys just a few rungs up from the bottom of the ladder.

Coasting past her nail salon, one foot riding the break, he saw Merrill's bottle-nosed Volvo parked up close to the front doors. He screeched to a near halt, then pulled across two lanes of traffic and into the lot. Blood thudded in his ears. "Calm down," he said out loud. He got out of his car and crossed the hot asphalt. There it was—the same beach pass, the roof rack, that scrape along the back fender. Peeping inside the rear windows, he saw a baby seat. His heart fell. Not hers. Up close he was surprised he had mistaken it; the car gave off signs of unfamiliar ownership. On the passenger side a newspaper was splayed out like a dead bird.

Straightening up, Osin caught his unkempt reflection in the window—his red-rimmed eyes and nose, the unshaven chin. His gray occipital hair waved nuttily in the breeze. He looked like his grandfather, who, in his eighties and with little to do except sit around, had suddenly declared bathing a waste of time.

Osin tracked down three other Volvos that afternoon, the last in the parking lot of Merrill's sports club. For at least twenty minutes he sat outside the building's front, watching the women frenetically racing on the treadmills. The gym was filled with young looking thirty and forty-year-olds like her. Even if she had been inside, he couldn't envision having a showdown where he'd be at such a clear disadvantage. With his heavy shoes and crumbling physique, Osin looked like a member of the Franklin Street Y next to the old folks' home.

Pulling onto Rt. 101, he realized he couldn't go home. The expanse of nighttime hours, the winking TV set, the glass of scotch, the silent bedroom—it was all so oppressive. He deliberated heading up the interstate just to hit a truck stop and have a meatloaf dinner. He was a sucker for these middle-class totems; they reminded him of his first marriage, and all the roasts, casseroles, and crockpot dinners he'd had. That was a time when women wore aprons, and Rosanna had one with a big carrot stitched onto it. She'd bustle around the kitchen, her hair tied up in a knot, her forgotten cocktail glass sweating on the counter. When they'd bought the house, she'd been thrilled with the kitchen and its pantry and cupboards, although by today's standards, it would be considered claustrophobic. Osin had repainted for her. Trying to remember the color he'd chosen, he found himself almost in Oakland, at Rosanna's. It had been at least fifteen years.

It was startling to see the old place again, to see that it existed as a real edifice separate from the shimmery refraction of his memory. He felt a strange pang, as he did when driving past an accident scene, the urge to look, the urge to turn away. The front walk was cracked, but Rosanna had put a new coat of yellow paint on the siding. The last time he was here was right after the divorce. He and Rosanna stood in the driveway screaming obscenities at each other, while their neighbor, old Ms. Battle, called in a trebly voice, "Who's over there? Is somebody hurt?"

The yard was kept up decently—nothing professional, the work of some neighborhood boys. The butterfly bush really needed to be cut back. Rosanna's rattletrap Honda was in the drive, and when he followed his line of sight up to the house, he saw her standing behind the screen door, watching him get out of the car and come up the walk. She'd gotten wider through her hips—the sediment had settled to the bottom of the glass.

"What are you doing home in the middle of the day?" he said. She had a scattered, leftist look, like a 1970s communist, or a recluse. Her gray hair had escaped the clip and flew all over the place. She was looking him over with those heavy-lidded eyes, one green, one blue, which had recessed like his with age. She'd opened the door but was holding her hand up, palm out, as if to say, "stop."

"Osin? What are you doing here?"

He halted under the shade of the awning. "Just a social call. I was in the neighborhood."

Her mouth was still slack with surprise, and the intimacy of that dark, exposed space bothered him.

"Well, aren't you going to let me in?"

The mouth closed. "I'd like to know what you're here for, first."

"Jesus, Rosie. Can't I just make a visit? Don't you ever get visitors? Or do you run them off the property with a shotgun?" It did look as if she were hiding something behind the door.

"You look awful, you know." She stepped back to let him in.

Inside the layout was just as he recalled it—narrow and low ceilinged, the close hallway hung with photographs and watercolors of the ocean. The center of the hall carpet was worn a lighter shade of blue. After he got over the initial pleasure of the familiar, he found it depressing that she'd never bothered to renovate. She went to make some coffee, and he wandered into the living room. With him gone, she had replaced his space with knickknacks that didn't fit into any particular decorating scheme— little ceramic animals and decorative plates, so many drink coasters. It was like a yard sale indoors.

"You really should replace this couch," he called to her. He pressed the faded cushion. One of the springs poked his hand. "I remember sitting on it."

"Why? It's fine."

"How many years have you had it? It's upholstery. It's not meant to last forever."

He strolled back into the kitchen. Over the pantry door, the cream paint had flaked, revealing the gypsum masonry underneath. The room reminded him of his Aunt Stella's apartment in Queens. He remembered then that he had pushed Rosanna, back when they were married, to rip out the old pine cabinetry and replace it with something more contemporary. "You never had the kitchen redone."

"Enough. It's not your life to criticize."

"It makes me feel guilty seeing this. Like I left you destitute after the divorce."

She handed him a decaf in a mug that said "World's Best Grandma." He tasted at least one shot of brandy.

The implacable silence bothered him. That wide back to him, his aunt's back. He hadn't gone back fifteen years in coming here; he'd gone back fifty. "I didn't leave you a pauper," he insisted. "I gave you plenty."

"I spent it all building a hospital. Then it folded."

He wasn't amused. Taking a seat at the chipped linoleum table, he looked down and noticed one ragged cuff flapping around his shoe. Where had he found these pants?

She sat down next to him with a pillowish thud. "Well, if this is a social call you might as well tell me how you've been."

A breeze came through the window above the sink, making the curtains flutter. She had African violets on the sill and one of those old-fashioned barometers—the woman in the sundress was out; the man with the umbrella was hidden indoors. Osin heard the sputtering of a car starting up down the street.

Then, without warning, Osin laid his head on the linoleum table and began crying in big, ugly sobs.

Rosanna shoved her chair forward. "Osin! You're not ill, are you?"

"Merrill left me."

"Oh," she said.

He cried on. It was uncontrollable, like urination. It went beyond Merrill, but he couldn't identify the cause. After a minute, he felt Rosanna's cool flat palm on his arm. He felt the skidding car that was himself, slow up. Come to a stop. Her voice floated somewhere near his ear. "It might not be for good. Give it some time."

Her response seemed to belong to the wrong scenario. He lifted his head and grabbed the offered tissue. What had that been, that darkness? He had lost the original thread of distress.

He returned to Merrill and the awful things she'd done. "She cheated on me." Rosanna was looking at him sympathetically, but she didn't seem appalled. "She's living with him," he added. He allowed himself to think of Merrill in the man's bed, her breasts pressed against his chest.

Rosanna didn't say anything. Osin followed her into the living room, talking about Merrill, that awful day she'd left, packing up her things, refusing to speak with him. Going through the cabinets. "She took the sugar even." Was that true? He was exaggerating, but it didn't seem to matter. Rosanna just sat there, saying nothing, and eventually he trailed off. That mortifying scene in the kitchen came back to him.

What had he expected? That she'd make up the sofa, run her fingers over his scalp, as she used to. Instead, they sat staring at each other. The clock ticked on, reminding him, in this house where time seemed to stop, that time had indeed passed.

"Well, I guess I should go home," he said.

"Are you all right to drive?"

He didn't feel like going outside where it was now night, where the saturated darkness pushed at the windows. As a boy, it was never under the bed he feared, but what lay outside the window, some loathsome oppressive dark, a shapelessness waiting to slide into his room. Even on the warmest nights he'd shut his windows before going to bed. His mother would come in the middle of the night and open them.

"How much liquor did you put in that coffee?" he asked Rosanna.

"Not enough to make a difference." She stood now, stolid, arms crossed over her upper chest like Renoir's Balzac. There was comfort there, but she wasn't going to provide it. But her defensive posture signified an internal war. It must be lonely for her, night after night. If he pushed her the right way, she might even let him in her bed. What would that be like? Pleasurable or horrific? Like the tale of the monkey's paw, where all the man's wishes arrived as tragedies, in perverted, terrifying forms.

But still, she was a woman with needs. He asked her tenderly, "Would you like me to stay?"

She started laughing. She started laughing so hard, her body pitched forward, and she covered her mouth with her hand.

"What's so funny about that?"

"Oh, Osin. I think it's best you go home. You'll be just fine."

With these generic words of comfort, she shut the door on him.

He woke up on his own couch, a sweated blanket twisted around his calf; he'd been dreaming about Merrill. She had worked at a dry cleaner and was taking his clothes with alarming speed. "Slow down," he shouted. He felt the words still dryly cluttering his mouth. Looking around he could make out the dim dimensions of the room. The blinds were closed, and it smelled stale and claustrophobic. The manicured digits of the stereo said ten-thirty a.m. Two inches from his face, Merrill's empty picture frame accused him. Osin heaved himself off the couch.

Stepping into the kitchen, he saw his dirty plates still in the sink from the day before. He felt a constrictive chill creep down his buttocks and the backs of his legs. He crossed the room and the cold sensation accelerated into panic. His heart began to race. What is wrong with me? His mind stopped with the thought—I can't wash the dishes. My hand is resting on the countertop, but I can't feel it. He suddenly pictured the high-speed nature film where a flower sprouts from the ground, blooms, and dies. It seemed as if he was going to fall forward, but he remained upright, taking slow, modulated steps out the kitchen, across the carpeted hall, and into the living room. He slid open a window, and the louvered blinds clacked. The sound reverberated in the room. He still felt that peculiar dizziness. Maybe he was having a heart attack. His brother Will had awoken one morning with chest twinges, a minor thing. Two days later both his legs were amputated. Osin would need to call an ambulance, but he couldn't focus; his head was filled with static. No, this feeling in his head, the buzzing, was probably a stroke. His brain was having a series of mini seizures. He breathed in, and the muscles in his chest tightened. He should go outside where there was more oxygen. With precise, cautious steps, an old lady crossing a frozen pond, he traversed the shifting floor to the terrace.

Sitting on the lawn furniture, he revived. His sweaty body was pleasantly chilled. He breathed in, let the air drop into his gut, and exhaled, watching the fat lips of the jade plants tremble next to him. Inhaling again, this time through his nose, he noted that his yard had no smell. The observation made him feel more like himself;

this would be something he'd think. A good sign—maybe the attack hadn't damaged too much of his brain. What had Rosanna's yard smelled like? Something sweet—jasmine, maybe. He should plant a bush, too. The house's menacing face stared at him. More than anything else, he just wanted to get out of there. He would have to go back inside, but only to get some things.

Like a child passing a graveyard, he took a deep breath and ran. He grabbed two suitcases, filling one with a few toiletries, a razor, shaving cream, and, he reminded himself, a bar of Lever—Rosanna probably used some kind of organic soap that didn't really clean you. He raced through the shelves trying to beat the slippery sensation coming up through his legs. He crossed Merrill's dressing room. A whole room to dress in—like a Vanderbilt! How could he ever have expected her to stay shackled to one man with all her fancy things? Emptied, it looked a little dingy, like the dressing room at an outlet store. The mirrored closets reflected him humping through.

When he drove up to Rosanna's, it was close to three. He admired the trimmed azalea bushes and the green lawns—a neighborhood of good hardworking people. Rosanna was getting into her little jalopy. He pulled up behind her, blocking the car in.

"Where are you going?" He walked over to her driver's side window. She was in a purple outfit—too fancy for errands.

"Osin! What are you doing here?"

"I think I may have had a stroke." Just uttering it made him want to break down. Again with the crying. It occurred to him, briefly, that the stroke might have damaged the nerve receptor that kept him from overreacting to emotional stimuli.

Rosanna reached her arm out the window and felt his head. "A stroke! Do you need to go to the hospital?"

"It happened twice. Both times in the house. At first I thought it was a heart attack." He described the sweating, the seizing up of his heart, vertigo, and the almost sure feeling of death, which he spoke about in metaphorical terms.

"I don't think that's a stroke. It sounds more like an anxiety attack."

"Why must you downplay everything? If I were to—" he hated saying it—"pass, you'd feel pretty terrible you'd sent me home."

She had taken her arm back into the car. "Why don't you see your doctor?"

"It's Saturday."

"Then I'll take you to the hospital. If you've had a stroke then you should be seen."

"I hate hospitals. Men my age go in for a minor thing and come out with a laundry list of ailments. Suddenly they're in there all day, waiting. Begging these rich doctors for two minutes of their precious time."

"I can see where the anxiety is coming from."

"So, you don't think it was a stroke?" He made a fist and released it. Left hand, then right. "I wouldn't be able to do that, would I? I would have neurological damage. Be dragging a leg."

"I still think you should be checked out. I'll drop you there."

"No, no. I'll wait until Monday. It was just a traumatic experience." He gave a short laugh, more like a bark. "The story of my week, I guess. It's nice here. That bougainvillea in bloom. Peaceful. But I'm still a little shaken up, so I thought, if you weren't doing anything, it would be nice to have someone else around."

"That's very sweet, but I'm going out."

"Where?"

She hesitated. "To Richard's. He's barbecuing."

To his own son's house! "And I'm not welcome?"

he said. Rosanna looked away, and he accused her, "You were just going to sneak out!"

"I wasn't sneaking. How was I supposed to know you were going to show up again? And since when do you see him on a non-holiday?"

"Jesus, I should have known life would hand me this. This shitty, miserable payoff. A lifetime of slogging and for what? Maybe it would be better to die here. Splayed out on the cracked blacktop of my ex-wife's house, while she's out enjoying herself, eating chicken legs at a barbecue with my son, laughing over—"

"Your morbid fantasies aren't helping. Negative thinking reduces your system's ability to fight off disease."

The sanctimonious bitch. He walked back to his car. She called out, "Look, if you really want to come, I can call over there and ask."

Osin said, "Don't knock yourself out."

"Fine," she said. "I'll call Judy."

"I'll wait out here." He leaned against the heated hood of the Mercedes. The breeze carried over the smell of swimming pool and grass clippings.

"I would suggest you take a shower first and shave," she said. "I really hope you brought other pants. Even yesterday I wondered if those were pajama bottoms."

II

Richard, his skinny, serious-minded boy, had turned into a middle-aged man overnight. He was wearing ill-fitting glasses that tinted to the level of sun, and a brown shirt. He looked as if he'd gotten taller, although that was impossible. How long had it been since they'd seen each other? At least six months. They had gotten along great until Ritchie turned thirty, married, and decided he suddenly had a bone to pick about his upbringing. Osin blamed the wife, Judy. It was in the nature of the frizzy-haired ones to be disagreeable. She began sizing Osin up right from the beginning, even before the wedding, when he made a good-natured joke about her big Irish feet. She'd responded through that long nose. "I don't appreciate your tone, Mr. Vachell." She was a good-looking woman, one of those lanky red heads with open hips like a ballet dancer's. She didn't have to be sweet; men would want to bed her anyway.

Coming over to him now, she limply offered up her face to be kissed. "How are you, Osin? This was unexpected."

He ignored the jab. "Yeah, well, I was around." He looked over her shoulder. "Hey there, Richard!" Every time he came near the boy, he felt a swelling in his chest. He stifled the urge to embrace him, instead settling for a hearty handshake.

Richard's hand was as wooden as a marionette's. "Hi, Dad," he said, and Osin realized that Ritchie was not pleased to see him.

The golden retriever thumped his feathery tail against Osin's legs. He'd gotten old too; he had a raccoonish white mask around the eyes.

They went around to the backyard, and Osin hung near Rosanna, his ally and a natural in this crowd. Just beyond the reach of the brick patio, his grandson, Bernard, was playing with some oversized plastic hardware. The boy's hair was even whiter now. He was so fair, he looked ill. When he came running over, Osin was surprised to see how tall he was—four years old, but he looked about seven. Bernard hugged his grandfather around the legs. His small hands fumbled at the seat of Osin's pants. After the kid disentangled himself, Osin checked his wallet. Still there.

Judy was showing Rosanna a blue bead necklace. "Isn't it beautiful? I have a friend in Palo Alto who makes them."

So, that's where Rosanna got her kooky style. When they were first married, she'd favored sweater vests, low-heeled pumps, and blouses with Peter Pan collars. Now she'd be just as apt to put on a sarong.

Osin went over to where his son was fiddling with the dials on the gas grill. "How are things going over here?"

Ritchie shook his head. He still had a good full head of hair. But there were worry lines in his face, and his posture wasn't confident. Financial troubles, probably. Richard was a recruiter for an employment firm—an unsteady boat to pile a family into. "From the looks of the place, you seem to be doing pretty well," Osin said. "Nice lawn, two cars in the driveway"—although one was a Ford.

"Things are fine," Richard said.

"Work?"

He shrugged. The wooden shoulders went up and down almost imperceptibly, like a flinch. "The market is looking up."

"Now what does that mean in your business, exactly? In the 'get rich quick' book business, sales went up when the economy went down."

He'd denigrated his own former line of work to give the boy an opening, but he shouldn't have bothered. Richard said, "Yeah, well, most of the world doesn't work like that. I have firms looking to fill more and more tech, and key marketing positions. I placed for three very big clients, recently, which netted a lot of cash."

"It must be tough, having your whole salary be commission like that." The idea of it made Osin wince. "Having to depend on that." He put his hand on his son's shoulder, which was tensed to resist him. Again he suppressed the rush of empathy. "Even though I'm retired, I have investments that did pretty well. Plus the house. So if you ever need anything, there's no shame in asking."

Richard said nothing. He had small, finely shaped hands, the Vachell hands, like Osin's own. As a kid Ritchie had always been painfully sensitive. Always worried about a test, or what a classmate said to him in the hallway. He'd work himself into tears this kid, sitting up at night, tracing out all the possible tragic outcomes. Some mornings he'd appear at the breakfast table with dark circles under his eyes. Osin had thought he was gay, then he had worried he had a mental disorder. He watched Richard's pale, delicate hands flip the meat. He hadn't turned out so bad, considering. He wanted to tell him, but instead he said, "You're probably wondering why I'm here alone. Merrill left me."

Richard's glasses had darkened to near opaque. "That's too bad," he said, as if Osin had lost his hat.

Sitting outside under the fading sun, their overcooked steaks in front of them, the three started gabbing about someone Osin didn't know. From what he understood, it was a neighbor with a lame foot, who had gone back into the hospital. Osin had nothing to contribute, and no one seemed to care, and so his mind began spinning off to Merrill's feet, her roughened instep, her piggishly round toes, which she usually kept polished. When she couldn't find something, she always checked under the couch cushions first. It was something he never understood. That, and the obsessive way she insisted on cleaning her own bathroom an hour before the woman came to do it. Did she even have a cleaning lady now? She was out living with that schlub in a dirty little house in Daly City. He must really be worth it. A two-bit realty manager dressed like an oversized teenager. White sneakers with a suit jacket! Osin should have suspected. Eventually it would appeal to Merrill's competitive nature to try and hook the boss. Osin gripped the bottom of his chair. But how would he have known! He had been duped by Eric's piss poor, commission-based salary and his awful haircut, the hangdog posture, and the lousy keyboard playing. You're a fool, he has youth, exuberance, a young penis. He cringed—Eric didn't take sex pills, or blood pressure pills, or spend half an hour on the toilet every morning. But he would eventually and then would Merrill leave him, too? Keep trading down and down until she reached junior high? And Osin would be alone. Dead or alone. She had squelched on the deal of togetherness. Osin complained once that the line at the bank was much longer than it used to be, and she, disgusted, had said, "You're like my father. Always comparing everything to the past."

"Grampy?" Bernard was trying to climb up on his lap. The boy's affection seemed pathological, as if he were prematurely weaned. Bernard's fingers were glistening with something. Honey? Osin shifted to make it difficult for him to settle.

"I made a picture." Bernard thrust an unidentifiable and slightly damp sketch in Osin's hands. "Look!"

"A heron?" Osin guessed.

Bernard climbed off without answering. Passing the dog, he grabbed its blubbery jowls between his hands and kissed it. Merrill would love this child. She couldn't have any herself because of a prolapsed uterus.

Osin tapped Judy on the knee. She started. He said, "Let me borrow Bernard tomorrow."

"Borrow?"

"He's my grandson. I want to spend some time with him. Take him to the park."

He expected, or hoped, that Rosanna was going to jump in and compliment him. She was annoyingly quiet, sipping her coffee.

"Well, he's got a play date," Judy sniffed.

"Ugh, that term." Osin shuddered. "Another sign the English lexicon has deteriorated. Believe me, he'll enjoy this outing more."

Judy looked pinch-faced, even in the flattering light from the hurricane lamp. She really was an unpleasant woman. Osin turned to Richard who appeared not to be listening; maybe he thought this type of scheduling was lady's business. "Ritchie," Osin said, "tell her how enjoyable spending time with me is."

"Osin!" Rosanna said.

He jumped. "What? I meant when he was a kid."

She shook her head quickly, like you'd do to a dog that was nosing in the garbage can.

"All right," Osin said to Judy. "Work me into Bernard's social calendar."

"He's not free until one." Judy stood up to clear the plates, ending the discussion.

Osin waited until he had Rosanna alone in the car. Then he said, "Thanks for sticking up for me back there!"

"I think you should tone it down a little. You can't expect to just breeze back into your son's life. Even I'm suspicious."

"Who's breezing back in? I just went over for a barbecue. Besides, it's not like anything terrible happened between us."

Rosanna shrugged.

"You think something's happened? Is that what he told you?"

"No, he hasn't said anything."

"Well, you don't really understand how men relate. Ritchie and I can get things back on track, now that I have time. That's one of the benefits of being retired."

They pulled into her driveway, where the crickets were singing. At his own house, the birds chirped at night, which he always found ominous.

Rosanna slammed the car door. "Good night."

"What? You're going to leave me here after the stroke?"

"I thought we agreed it was a panic attack."

"We agreed nothing. It was excruciating." Even now the thought of his house gripped him like a python. When had his mind decided to equate the house with such despair, with this nauseating emptiness? It didn't matter, the association was made. "Look—" He grabbed Rosanna's arm. "I need you to let me stay. Just one night. I can sleep in the guest room or something. Whatever you want. I just need you to let me stay, and I need you to not ask me a chain of questions why. Please, Rosie. *Please.*"

After the humiliating expression of all this need, the deal was made. Women frequently demanded these excruciating confessions of vulnerability—it's the price they exact for their companionship. It was always a toss-up, whether to give in or walk away. He had hoped to sleep in Richard's old room, if the twin mattress was still up there, but Rosanna didn't offer. Maybe she didn't trust him being on the same floor with her. Instead, she fixed his bed on the couch with a bottom sheet and a thin blanket. When he rolled onto his side, he felt a spring poke him in the ribs.

"Okay," she said. "Sleep well." She was holding back with him, he could sense it. He watched her ghostly white ankles ascend the stairs. He slept soundly, having, for the time being, evaded the terrors that worked on him in solitude.

The next morning he arrived at Richard's ten minutes early. Judy and Bernard were already waiting for him in the kitchen. He hadn't noticed it last night, but the room was decorated in a faux country-style with Pennsylvania gift shop goods. The table was one of those pine plank ones with stenciled blue hearts trimming the leg. He looked around for Richard. "Where's my son?"

"It's a weekday," Judy said. "He works."

She was dressed in a flowy white garment that indicated she planned on going with them. He said, "You know it's just going to be me and the kid, right?"

She frowned, and Osin turned to Bernard, who was fiddling with the loose knob on a cabinet door. "You look better than you did the other day. More with it. Nice jacket."

Bernard tugged his mother's hand all the way down the driveway. Osin could tell from Judy's squinted eyes that she was considering calling the trip off. He rapidly loaded Bernard's bags of traveling gear into the Mercedes's trunk. "This kid has enough luggage for a hotel stay."

"He's not leaving until you tell me what your plans are."

"The aquarium. What's this?" Osin picked up Bernard's insulated lunchbox. "I was going to spring for his meal."

"You're going all the way to San Francisco?"

"You act like it's miles away. It's just over the bridge."

Mimicking a valet, Osin opened the front door for Bernard with a short bow. The kid started climbing up, and she hauled him back. "Are you crazy? He's four!"

She went back to the Volkswagen and got out the car seat. It reminded Osin of medical surplus, a wheelchair with a padded armrest and cup holder. It had to be set up in the back seat, not the front. "Well, put him where I can see him," Osin said. "It's already going to kill conversation if I have to talk to him through the rearview."

Backing out of the driveway, Osin saw Bernard's pale, apprehensive face strain to get a last glimpse of his house. Then, through the mirror, he and Osin locked eyes. Bernard's were as big and brown as a frightened dog's. "Don't worry," Osin said. "You're in for a good time."

The additional person in the car was somehow comforting. Osin tipped his head back to listen to Bernard's shallow breathing. Below the Bay Bridge, the sailboats were drifting by on the roughened, white-peaked water. Bernard reached toward the window, as if they were toys he could catch. Once they reached the San Francisco side, Osin pulled over in a windy turnaround and took out a t-shirt he had made up yesterday at the mall. In block letters it said, "I forgive you." On the back it said, "For cheating. Come home."

"What's that?" Bernard asked. Osin tugged the shirt over Bernard's head. It was too big, more like a dress. The folds would probably obscure the lettering. He'd been tempted to stop at "I forgive you," but then, at the last moment, he added the additional phrases. Knowing Merrill, and her capacity for self-forgiveness, she'd come back as if she'd done nothing wrong.

"What's that say?" Bernard asked again, pulling at the shirt. Osin noticed the kid repeated himself a lot.

"We're going to send a message," Osin said. "Can you read?"

Bernard was suddenly fired up. "Yes. I know these words, cat, and uh, bicycle—"

Osin turned back to the wheel. "You know that only a year or two after you start reading, your teeth fall out."

"What?" Bernard said.

The open house was in Noe Valley, an area of the city Osin was less than familiar with; it took him a while navigating the hilly streets to find the place. His throat caught when he saw Merrill's Volvo in the driveway. Blue and yellow agency balloons were tied to her sign.

She was still using his last name, or maybe she was just too cheap to have new signs made up.

He unbuckled Bernard from his special seat. The kid's hair smelled sour, like turned milk. Gripping his grandson's hand, Osin approached the front door, which appeared to be hand-carved mahogany. This house would certainly turn a nice profit for the keyboardist. Let it be a farewell gift. Once Merrill moved back in, she'd have to find another agency to hand her profits to. He and Bernard went inside.

That morning Osin had spent some time in Rosanna's tiny bathroom, practicing his cold smile in the mirror. The grave, reprimanding eyes, the lips that stretched humorlessly across the face. It was the look of rebuke, and it disarmed Merrill, usually provoking a series of her nervous, scrambled questions. He would be magnanimous, but only after her initial apology. He would let go of any resentment and never speak of her straying again.

With a cold drop in his gut, he spotted Merrill. She was bent over a folding table, flipping through a stack of papers. He recognized the small rise of her shoulder blades, the outline of her narrow rear beneath her red suit, the same suit she wore on her business cards. He saw the tips of her ears protruding slightly from the blown-out hair. It had been lightened again to the shade of beach sand.

"Hello," he said. Bernard's hand felt slick and limp in his. "I'm looking for a smaller place."

She looked up, and before she opened her mouth, he saw, in those serene, motionless eyes, her failure to recognize him.

He felt a pinching sensation and looked down. Bernard was gripping at his leg near the crotch, like a monkey clinging to a tree. Osin pulled the pants' fabric out of his hands.

Merrill's lips were pressed together angrily.

He began again. "I've—"

She bent down to Bernard. "Who's this?" she said, in her liquid, salesy voice. Like the bedroom voice, it was meant to ease you out of your fretted conscious mind. "Bernard? You've gotten big."

"Introduce yourself," Osin told him. The kid was making a weird anxious sound. He buried his face in Osin's upper thigh. Osin patted his head. "He's a little shy of you."

Merrill stood up. "I'm not going to ask you why you've come. Whatever the reason, it's incredibly inappropriate."

"I've come to see the house," he insisted miserably. "I'm thinking of investing in real estate here."

"No. No way."

"I believe it's in your professional code to show me the place. Not to discriminate."

She had rimmed her eyes with kohl, which gave her an exotic look. Those flat, glass blue eyes—emotionless, mesmerizing. Her lips pushed out farther. Then, just as quickly, she said, "All right."

Her words sent another wave of anxiety through him.

Once he was knee-deep in his charade, however, he started to relax. She took them on a clipped tour of the rooms, spitting out her realty facts. Her voice went up and down the musical register, but it was a poor act, devoid of sentiment. He lagged behind, pretending to admire the molding. It actually wasn't a bad place. Two levels, floor-to-ceiling windows, partial views of the city, and 2.5 baths. When she walked past the second bathroom, he corrected her. "I'd like to see this, as well."

He hoped she'd step into the bathroom with him, but she stayed in the doorway. "These tiles are imported from Italy." She pointed to the sink. "They stay. These fixtures, unfortunately, go."

"It's very nice," he said, "but probably overpriced at one point eight."

"In this market you'd be lucky if you're not outbid offering full." She refused to look at him, and still, it was unnerving being this close to her. He felt effervescent, on high speed. And to think he'd spent years waking up to her every morning, watching her brush her teeth and slump around in her garish nightgowns. He'd listened to her rattle on about this or that property and who'd come in and out. She never had a storyteller's grace—all details from the fascinating to the mundane received equal billing. How bored he'd been. Yet here, meekly descending the staircase after her, he felt his rusty knees buckling with exhilarated panic.

Bernard had detached himself from Osin's grip and was spinning around the kitchen. Stopping near the granite island, he stumbled and said, "Whoa."

This was clearly the end of the tour, and Osin said, "So, I thought that we—"

Merrill rudely turned her back. "Bernard," she said. "Your shirt's so big. It's like a man's shirt."

Osin started. The message, the shirt, belonged to the script they'd thrown out in the first five minutes.

Paralyzed, he watched as she bent down to Bernard, who looked up in alarm. "Lemme see," she said, stretching out the material, reading the front, then the back.

She straightened up. In a whisper that Osin mistook, at first, for intimacy, she said, "Get the fuck out."

Once he was buckled back in the car, Bernard let out a stream of talk about horses, and something named Bill that Osin at first thought was a school friend but turned out to be a pet. He began chaining together partial memories of his father fixing up an antique car, which Osin suspected of being untrue. Blocks later and Bernard was still chattering away to his window like a sprung canary.

Through the swampy mess of his own thoughts, Osin said, "I think I liked it better when you were scared to speak."

Bernard grabbed his stomach. "Ha! Ha! You're funny."

In the aquarium parking lot, Bernard started throwing a tantrum when Osin tried to remove the shirt. He flailed around in his car seat, lifting his arms to prevent it from being slid off his head. Osin was gutted enough from his recent experience not to put up a fight. He led Bernard, in his accusatory outfit, to the concrete fortress.

"There are thousands of gallons of water in here," he said. What it would take to design a building as structurally intricate between these walls as a bridge—a whole network of interlocking cables and beams. He was oppressed with the thought of it. The disgust on Merrill's face, it was the same way she looked when describing a particularly stupid buyer. As if he were the one who'd cheated and had come to beg her forgiveness.

In the touching pool Bernard grabbed first at the starfish, and then just at the water, letting it drip from his fingers again and again until Osin, fed up, said, "Okay, you want to see the sharks? You seen sharks before?"

"Oh, sure," Bernard answered in a surprisingly deep voice. "They have mouths on their neck. To breathe." Osin felt him reaching for his hand. Were they lost? The aquarium seemed to have the spaciousness of the sea itself. The two of them traversed the massive aqua hallways, looking for the sharks.

In the large tank, teeming with other aquatic life, they watched a hammerhead swim slowly by, passing them and then returning, like a runner on a track. Bernard gripped the railing. A skate sifted past Osin's head. How could he have misjudged her so completely? She acted as if they had no history, as if he were an obsessive stranger, fulfilling some aberrant urge. He felt a blistery shame rise up through his face. She had looked fantastic. Her new life, her adultery, had given her a horrid grandeur. Since when had she cursed at him without breaking down in tears first?

It wasn't until later that evening that he realized this was the same Merrill, now inflated with the exhilaration of wronging him. He had tried to approach her on his own level, as her husband. If he wanted to win, he'd have to go at the Merrill that sat atop her high horse.

He tapped Rosanna while they were sitting in the kitchen having tea. He was hooked on three cups a day now, heavily sweetened. She'd make him a diabetic if he stayed around much longer.

"So," he said to her. "You're a woman, although a mature woman. Tell me how to get Merrill back."

"I would prefer to talk about your staying here. I see you brought another suitcase."

"I needed clean underwear. And an alarm clock. Yesterday I was almost late to Richard's." He paused. "While I was back at my house, I also looked around for clues as to why Merrill went bad."

"Why do you need an alarm clock? You told me you were only going to stay for one night. "

"Why are you harping on that! I'm only asking for another night. And I brought us some steaks to thank you with." He pointed to the refrigerator. "I'll cook them."

"Osin, you need to be dealing with this. This fear, or whatever it is. You can't just run away from your house because it reminds you of some failing. I would be no friend to you if I just let this go on. Here—" She went over to one of the three junk drawers in the kitchen cabinetry, and fished out a piece of paper and a pen, missing its cap. She scribbled down a phone number and thrust it at him.

He read it. "I already have a doctor. One of the best in the Bay Area. I doubt this guy is better."

"She's a therapist. Someone for you to talk to."

Osin quietly folded the paper and put it in his back pocket.

"Well?" she said.

"Are you going to make it conditional for my stay?"

"I never agreed to this 'stay'."

"I don't understand, because if the purpose of this therapy is to have someone to tell my problems to, then I'm sitting right here, trying to tell you what is wrong in my life, and you won't listen."

"You need someone impartial, to extract the real problem from the thing you're choosing to obsess over."

"You're impartial. You tell me what is really wrong. My age, my death, etcetera." He leaned in closer to her, clasping his hands in a steeple. "I just don't understand how I didn't see this coming. That Merrill could go from good wife to lousy bitch all of a sudden."

"Usually it's a slower process than that."

"Well, I didn't see it. And when I went back to the house, all I found were some farty old sweaters and those cheap romance novels she likes. They encourage dissatisfaction. It's the cliffhanger structure, something better is always going on in the plot line you just left off. But it seems a bit of a stretch to see that as the reason she left. Tons of housewives read those books." He sighed. "I should have plugged her for answers when I had the chance."

"If you've gotten over your anxiety enough to sit in the house and read a book, maybe you should try spending a night there."

"I'm not over it! It took me a half an hour just to get out of the car. And I could only make it as far as the living room. It was stifling. I barely made it out in time."

"All right. No need to get upset." She patted his hand condescendingly. "This is why a professional would better for you."

"Look, Rosanna, I'm asking for your help here. Stop trying to duck out of it. Something happens to me when I'm in that house. I feel squeezed, like I'm in the grip of some large malevolent force. It's humiliating. I hate it. And I need to get over it. But in the meantime, I need a place to stay. I want to stay here. Not at an anonymous hotel." He realized he'd been grasping the edge of the table so hard, his hands ached. He folded them in front of him again. "Your influence could be good for me."

She opened her mouth, and he rushed on, "I'm not bullshitting you. It feels right for me to be here." And if she should refuse? Would he sleep in his car? Would he check himself into a sanitarium? "I'll pay you whatever you want. It might be nice to have a little extra income. I'll follow all your rules. No questions asked. I just need to stay. Please don't make me enumerate the times I've helped you—I'm trying to work on my pettiness."

His breath was short with the effort. His heart beat heavily, as if his blood were viscid.

She said, "This won't be forever, right? Just a temporary thing?"

"Absolutely. Thank you. You're very good." Giddy with relief, he added, "You may even enjoy yourself, you know. We could have a great time. You've always found me something of a wit. I say the things you think."

"I disagree with almost everything that comes out of your mouth. But you are amusing, either by accident or design." She smiled. "I've never heard you speak this much about your feelings."

"It's Merrill." He recounted the open house, leaving out Bernard. "And then I was on the verge of telling her I wanted her back, and she kicked me out!"

"What were you expecting?" Rosanna got up and began taking the dishes out of the drying rack. He was still amazed at all the things she didn't own, a computer, a dishwasher, a DVD player.

"This isn't a carnival act," she said. "She's at her workplace. You need to be selective with your timing."

"Well, it's done. What should my next step be?"

She closed the cabinet. "It doesn't look good."

"What kind of cheerleader are you? Just when I'd gotten my spirits up."

"You could write her a letter, I guess. You're good with words."

"A letter! Even I know how old-fashioned that is. That's how my father courted. Merrill already knows I'm old. That's the problem."

"People still write letters. And it would give you time for reflection. Some self-editing."

"What the hell would I say in it? She knows the details."

"You could start by apologizing for that scene in Noe Valley, for one. Use that as an entryway for some flattery. Tell her you've been doing some thinking. That you want her to be happy."

"She already looks happy. She's getting fat off her own good times."

"Well then lie." Her one blue eye looked him over. "I would avoid going off the deep end into your own feelings of injustice, anger, and all the rest. It's not winning material."

Osin watched her walk across the kitchen. There was a lot of torso movement. When he noticed it the other day at Richard's, he'd assumed it was just the unevenness of the turf. She had been walking with one hand flippered out, like a seal. For balance? Merrill walked a straight line, her rear thrust out, so everyone could admire it. He thought of the dimple at the top of

Merrill's ass, and then the two creases where it met the thighs. He felt a nostalgic throbbing in his groin. Eric was probably rubbing his hands over that ass right now. They could even be having a quickie while he sat here in Rosanna's kitchen sipping her old maid's tea. Black heat rushed into his chest.

"Scoff all you want," Rosanna was saying. "A woman in my garden club took her husband back when he wrote her a long letter. And he was in much worse shape than you."

"Your garden club! I can only imagine what a donkey that woman was." Osin drummed the table. "Merrill is *attractive.* She's forty-two. She has options."

"You want another example? How about your own son. He writes Judy a love note every morning before he goes to work."

"He does?" His son always was a needy kid, afraid of being left behind. But still, it was surprising—Ritchie certainly wasn't going overboard with affection at the cookout. "I didn't know he went in for that type of uxoriousness. You've got to admit, even you think that's overkill."

"He's happily married."

Osin sighed. "I miss Merrill. We had our good times."

"Be prepared," Rosanna said. "You'll miss her a lot. Especially when you're tired. And if you get sick."

Out of gratitude, and because Rosanna's housekeeping was occasionally slip-shod, Osin dusted all the living room trinkets one morning. Then he got out a mangy looking sponge mop and washed the floor. He waited all afternoon for her to notice, and when she didn't, he pointed it out.

"That reminds me," she said. She handed him a chore list. "Here's your list of responsibilities."

"This is like a halfway house. *Clean the toilets!* Why can't you give me something more masculine, like outdoor work?"

"Because I know how to garden, and you don't. And you said you cleaned this morning, so I don't understand what the problem is."

"But I don't want to make a profession out of it." He tapped the page. "Dusting is on here again? I doubt you've been sticking to this once-a-week schedule. There was at least a two-month coating of dust on top of the television."

"This sounds a lot like the backtalk you swore not to give me," she said. Behind that comment, he was meant to understand, was the threat of expulsion. She looked at him meaningfully.

"All right. Fine. Forgive me for speaking up. I'll dust."

Instead what he did was make a phone call to Asmarina, his Russian housekeeper, and booked her for the Wednesday morning that he knew Rosanna was at her gardening class. He let Asmarina in. "You think you can get this done in two hours?"

She was a short, thick-limbed woman with pinned up gray hair and a no-nonsense attitude. Osin had a feeling she liked him, although he wasn't sure why. His life must seem frivolous to her. She didn't ask any questions, such as why he was here. "This is a small house. Okay, I can do in two hours. Not perfect, but good."

"Not the whole house, just these things." He got out the list. "Mop the living room, but not the kitchen. The kitchen's her job." He went around pointing it out. It took her less than an hour. It would have taken Osin all afternoon. "I'll call you about next week," he said, pressing the money into her hand.

"You still want me to clean in Marin?"

"Yes. It looked great last time I was there. Thanks."

Rosanna noticed immediately. "It looks fantastic in here! And I can't believe you're done already—you had until the end of the week."

"I like to clean when you're out at your class. I don't want you to see me down on my hands and knees scrubbing. It's emasculating."

"Well, you really did a superior job. Much better than last time. You even did the baseboards."

"Okay, enough gushing. What's for lunch?"

"What's for lunch? Make yourself something! This isn't preschool."

He wondered sometimes, especially in the late afternoons, whether he wasn't a kept man. Oil prices were rising, men were making energy deals, the tech industry was booming again and outsourcing overseas, and here he sat in the mausoleum of Rosanna's living room with the cloying scent of windowsill geraniums everywhere. She probably enjoyed having him around, castrated and smiling, not saying a word against her for fear of being ejected into the street. A docile houseguest was even better than a husband.

He caught the end of Stephen King's *Misery* on cable, and then went out and bought the book. There was a sadistic streak in the most unlikely women, and it was expressed in the domestic sphere. Wasn't Rosanna using her home against him? Making him a prisoner by fulfilling his need to stay? Where was Merrill? By some cruel, unforeseeable turn, the Italian leather chair that he should be sitting in had disappeared. The book, the curtains, the woman, they were all wrong. Low-grade replacements had been subbed in.

"What are you reading over there?" Rosanna asked. She was on the couch with yet another Austen novel. "Stephen King! I didn't know you liked horror."

"Sometimes," he said.

"Well, I'm going to put the kettle on. Do you want tea?"

He stood. "Since I'm still able to use my legs. I'll get it."

"That's nice of you. Just one sugar. I'm trying to cut back."

"I'm putting a little whiskey in mine. Would you like a shot in yours?"

"In tea?"

"Sure, why not? This reform house doesn't have any rules against alcohol, does it?" Rosanna guzzled wine like she could turn it into water. "The trick is not to let the bag seep too long. Lemon and orange pekoe are best. Chamomile's not bad. Even peppermint's ok. But then you're better off going with rum."

"That's disgusting," she said. "You have the unique ability to make even the healthiest things unhealthy."

He was tempted to say something nasty, but held back. All of this repression would put him in an early grave. He needed to get out of here and back to his own home, his life, his wife, the world he had traded up for fifteen years ago, and moved about in with the ease of sovereignty. Let Rosanna go back to suffering her loneliness. "Suit yourself," he told her and went into the kitchen.

That night, after Rosanna went to bed, Osin began his letter. *Dear Merrill, my wife and friend, the only woman who has ever understood me. I'll forgive everything if you come back. We've both made a terrible mistake. We were supposed to grow old together.* No, no. He crossed that out. *I love you. Eric doesn't. Men that look sensitive usually only care about themselves.* This was a truth, but probably one she wasn't ready for. *Remember when we went to Bermuda? You said you had never been so happy. Forget the scene at the open house the other day. I shouldn't have gone there. I*

*wish I'd asked you more about the affair, but I was unpre-
pared to handle your response. I still don't want to know
why you left. I just want you to come back. I never wrote
you a note each morning to tell you that I loved you, but I
thought it. Our home misses you and so do I. Love, Osin.*

The mail would take too long. Should he have Rosanna
drop it off? She'd probably refuse, or she'd say yes, then
lose it in the mess of her car. She kept all sorts of garbage in there—plastic bags, pamphlets, even a little stool
someone had left out on the curb.

That night he got in the Mercedes and drove over to
Eric's. He had some trouble finding it. A year ago, when
Merrill first signed on with the realty agency, they'd
come out here for an awful, cheap party. Potato chips
and Cheez-its had been served in big, communal bowls.
And then Eric, still wearing his ridiculous white sneakers, got behind his keyboards and hammered out Jimmy
Buffet covers, while they all sat in agony. Osin gripped
the steering wheel. Merrill had agreed. "What an idiot,"
she'd said.

Osin pulled up to the address. It was a lousy house
for a house salesman. Two-story and a non-descript sand
color, which looked sickly under the distant glare of the
streetlamps. There was only one small, penitentiary window facing the front. Osin remembered that at the party,
he'd heard a scraping noise, like someone sideswiping
his new car. He'd gone from room to room desperately
trying to find a window.

He looked down at his watch—it was now after
twelve, and no lights were on. Eric had given them a tour
at that party, as if the house were a mansion, and Osin
remembered seeing a bedroom on the first floor. Around
the side of the house, he deliberately trod on the petu-
nias and the neat row of hostas, hearing the satisfying
crunch of the stems. Would he be able to stomach seeing

them sleeping together, or worse, having sex? Grasping the sill, he looked in. His breath caught. Merrill was curled up in a little ball, and Eric was lying behind her, his hairy hands cupping her breasts. Or was that a leg? Osin squinted. Were they having sex from behind? She always liked that position—he should have known how depraved she was. No. As his eyes adjusted to the darkness, he saw that Merrill's torso was actually a cat lying on one of those husband pillows, a crumpled up blanket, and a stack of file folders. Even after the cat got up and left the room, he was still squinting into the darkness.

His heart was beating enough to explode. They must be sleeping upstairs. A crazy wildness in his chest told him to break in through a window, kicking over lamps and night tables, and threaten them with something— that baseball bat he kept in the trunk. But what type of humiliation, and possible beating, would he be in for if he lost his nerve midway through? Even naked, Eric could quickly take him.

Quiet and quick-footed, he made his way around to the front door, which was crowded with sinisterly over-grown shrubbery. A little metal mailbox hung, tenement style, from the shingle. Osin laid the envelope down in the center of the welcome mat. As a precaution against it blowing away, he secured it down with a stone.

He waited all the next morning for his cell phone to ring. At noon he remembered the house and called to check the messages there. There was one hang-up caller. He listened to the click and dial tone three times to see if he could hear any identifiable breathing. Nothing. At around mid-afternoon, it occurred to him that Merrill might go by the house in Marin. Osin snuck out the back door and got in the car. He was almost at the end of the block when he decided he was being ridiculous. He pulled over and called Merrill.

She answered on the second ring, and he jumped in, "I left you a letter last night. You may not have gotten it—"

"I got it," she said.

He waited.

"I'm sorry." Her voice was thick with arrogance. "I don't know what to say that hasn't already been said. I don't want you sneaking around the house late at night. It's creepy."

"You should think things over. We're married, for Christsake." His hands were trembling like an old woman's. What shame.

"I have thought it over." She lowered her voice. "Understand it's for the best. I never saw you—"

"Because I was working? Well, I'm not working now. I have time for you."

"It's not that. We're just not really well suited."

Where had she gotten this language from? "Of course we are. Otherwise we wouldn't have gotten married!"

"Osin, you're going to force me to be unkind. I hate myself like that. Listen, I forgive you for showing up at my open house. It's okay."

"But you need to explain it to me. Why you left."

"Again! I can't keep going through this. Keep reliving it. You need to accept. Our relationship is over. It's been over. I don't owe you anything anymore. Stop acting like I do."

There was a point, he realized, when he needed to block out what she was saying. Mentally record it to examine later, but block it out for now. If he didn't, he would be unable to continue on the phone. The pain was much greater than he imagined.

There was a bearish cough in the background. "Where are you?" he asked.

"I'm at home, Osin."

"Home? Home is our house in Marin."

"At some point you're going to have to accept that Eric and I—"

Osin hung up.

A few hours later, sitting in a bar in the seedier section of San Francisco, he started wondering how he had not seen that their marriage had these submerged problems. They'd seemed happy. They dined out and complained about the service. They went to a movie, and he knew what to buy her at the concession stand. He knew how much of the box of M&M's she'd eat before saying she'd had enough, and then sneaking the rest from where it was hidden in her purse. How greatly he had been able to deceive himself, thinking he'd been tolerating her habits. How he'd patted himself on the back for over-looking that she bored him. She didn't have a good eye for detail. She never seemed to know if something was bothering him until days after he was over it, and then, belatedly, she would pester him with questions. These were large-scale issues too, consolidations at the pub-lishing house and financial worries. Whole weeks he walked around with the oppressive fear of losing his job, and his wife still had no idea. Merrill had never seemed a worthy vessel to dump his troubles into. She would get very nervous, and that would cause her to be selfish, worrying aloud how this was going to affect their income. When she calmed down, her suggestions usually involved the manipulation of his colleagues' sympathies. Her dishonest streak troubled him. She'd butter up a buyer, cheating another agent out of the split. To get out of being a bridesmaid on the day of her friend's wedding, she'd lied and said her mother had gone into the hospital.

Through the smeary window, Osin watched a soused bum try to slump against a tree. That man looks like me, he thought. Had he reached the age where he started looking indistinguishably elderly? Merrill would probably ask him for a divorce. He sipped his bourbon and soda, his father's drink.

By the time he got back to Rosanna's, it was past eleven. She had left the outside light on and the door unlocked.

He didn't speak to Rosanna all the next morning. Why had he taken advice from a woman who had failed in her own bid to lure him back? Osin stayed up in his old study, now a spare bedroom. The entire house reminded him of a time when his income was much lower.

He didn't see Rosanna until mid-afternoon when she passed by carrying a piled laundry basket. Through the open doorway, he called out, "Well, that was a mistake! You're as out of touch as I am."

She continued towards the stairs, so that he had to get up and follow her into the hall. "I expected you to keep your own counsel until dinner," she said over her shoulder.

"I wrote your letter—"

She put the basket down. "What did it say?"

"Don't worry. I put plenty of *feelings* in it. It practically stood up and sobbed. That's not why this idea stunk." His face got hot even thinking about it. How many times had he used the word "love," blubbering all over the page. "What happened? I'll tell you—nothing! And when I called—"

"I don't remember advising you to call."

"I had to do something! I didn't get a response."

"She was probably still thinking it over. God knows what you put in there."

"No. She was never going to answer it. I knew this was a bad idea. So passive. Writing is too passive. It's asking to be ignored."

"You can't bully her into moving back in, Osin. You gave it your best shot. At least now she knows how you feel."

"Yeah, sure. That's a comfort." He turned back to his room. "You know, some people are just meant to be doormats for others."

Rosanna bent over to pick up a stray sock. "Are you talking about Merrill or me, now?"

"I'm talking about myself. You remember how passive my father was. He was always telling me not to fight a woman. When I was ten, I saw my mother smack him right across the jaw. For what? Nothing probably. Maybe he was late getting home. That stuck with me in a subliminal way my whole life."

"Of all the fictions you tell yourself this one is above and beyond. A doormat! You've had an aggressive life, an avaricious one."

"I don't believe that." He shook his head. "If I had, things would have turned out much different."

"They haven't turned out that badly. You have a wonderful, big house you're not living in with—"

"Why do you keep talking about that! You really know how to kick a man when he's down!" He went back into his room, slamming the door.

A few hours later he'd decided to forgive Rosanna and went downstairs to tell her. He found her in the living room redressed in a pale linen suit, a long necklace, and flats. Always flats. She probably hadn't worn a pair of heels in twenty years.

"That's not a bad outfit," he said. "Classy. Lose the kooky beads and you'll look ten years younger."

"I'm going out to visit a friend who's in the hospital." She unclasped a small pocketbook and put her wallet in. This was not her everyday purse, which was big, brown, and stuffed with newspaper clippings, a broken robot toy, and used tissues. He'd fished through it while she was outside gardening.

"It must be a special visit for you to leave your junk behind," he said.

"I see that late day nap didn't cure your nasty disposition."

How did she know he'd slept? He rubbed at his cheek. "So what's wrong with your friend?"

"She's had a hysterectomy. But there were some complications."

"The tricky female organs. You're going to stop for flowers on the way, I assume."

She took a pair of scissors out of the end table drawer and held them up. "The callas have bloomed. And I'm bringing her a banana bread."

"We have banana bread here?"

"I assume that means you'll be staying in while I'm out." She looked over at where he had slumped down on the couch, a pair of used socks shoved into the cushion next to him. "You know it isn't healthy for you to sit around like this."

"I'm cleaning, aren't I?"

"I was talking about a hobby." From the brown purse, she fished out pamphlets from the California Trails Office. "I picked these up for you."

"Why?"

"The parks need people to clean up. It's an opportunity for you to get out. Get some fresh air, meet people, and make yourself useful."

"Doing sanitation work?"

"A lot of it is clearing trails of invasive plants. I thought you'd be interested. You always liked the outdoors. Better than just sitting on my couch all day, eating chips. Which I see you bought. You know I don't allow junk food in my house."

"I'm allowed to buy my own groceries."

"It would be good for you. As people get older they become more prone to depression. Especially with the sedentary lifestyle you're leading."

"Terrific. I'm sure that good cheer will go over well at the hospital."

Her eyes swept the room. "Don't answer the phone. And try and remember to put the milk back in the fridge, please."

After she left, he wandered around, unsure of what to do with himself. Maybe he should read; there were certainly enough books here. He had always preferred the American classics, Melville and Thoreau. Most of his career had been spent with books, and yet he'd never had time to read. Had been—it was difficult to think in those terms.

His old basketball trophy was still in the corner hutch. Pictures of him and Rosanna, and the three of them as a family, hung on the walls ascending the staircase. Richard, looking undernourished in his gym shorts and big glasses, stood alone by a rock in some unidentifiable locale. Osin felt a tightness in his throat seeing the kid's hesitant posture. Soon after that picture was taken, Osin had moved out.

He went up the stairs. The heavy lacquer had worn off the banister in the high-use places, revealing a slick, light-colored surface. He was headed for their old bedroom, but was stopped by a photo of Rosanna's friend Susan Liffey in her crotch-hugging shorts. It was taken on their camping trip to the Grand Tetons. He stood beside her, shaggy-haired and virile, holding a stack of firewood. He remembered how excited he had been sneaking Susan, late at night after everyone had gone to bed, down the dirt path, and giving it to her against the side of a tree. The pine needles against the soles of his feet, the dark woods, Susan's heated body, all of it—incredible. That weekend, eyeing Susan across the picnic table, felt like nothing else. When he dropped something, she'd spread her legs to give him a view.

In the photo, Rosanna stood on his other side with her brown pageboy and a game smile, squinting up at the camera. He didn't remember much of her from that trip. He searched himself for guilt, but the most he could come up with was a nagging sense that he'd acted badly. Had shown bad character. Guilt was hard to muster; it usually went along with regret, and he couldn't regret this experience. He had enjoyed it too much. Even now, the memory produced a rush of pleasure—wasn't that the supreme purpose of life, for which half remains unlived, the other half remembered?

Then it occurred to him—Merrill, that adulteress, probably felt the same. Had she been thinking about him at all when she went after Eric? The situation suddenly took horrid, precise shape. She enjoyed fucking Eric. She didn't want to be liberated. Osin pictured her having sex in Eric's shower stall. She could be giving Eric a blowjob right now in the chair where Osin had sat and eaten his chips.

He had to know. His hands shaking, he rang Merrill. This time she didn't answer.

When Rosanna came in three hours later, he was sitting at the kitchen table. "What's wrong?" she said. "You look awful." She noticed the cell phone still gripped in his hand. "Did you get bad news?"

"I've been doing some thinking." He had calmed considerably. "It's an unpleasant reality, but now I know how you felt being cheated on. It really is a sickening experience."

"Yes, it is. But I always knew you had problems. That made it slightly easier." She started unpacking her groceries. He could tell by the colors of the labels that some were store brand. "That poet was an awful woman. It didn't feel that great to be passed over for a woman who talked out of the side of her mouth like a bad ventriloquist. You could barely understand her."

"Gail?" said Osin. "I forgot about her." She had a pale, wintry look that was sort of beguiling. But very shy—she never looked at you dead on. The shy ones were supposed to be real firecrackers in the bedroom. So much for that myth.

"Who were you talking about?"

"Susan."

"Susan?" Rosanna froze, a jar of tomato sauce in her hand. "Who's that?"

Osin hesitated. "Forget it. I was just trying to make a point. When Merrill was sneaking over to Daly City to be with that rat tail, Eric, I thought I was going to lose my—"

"Wait a second, Susan Liffey? My friend from Oneonta?" The lid above her blue eye twitched.

"I thought you knew," he said, lamely.

"Why the hell would I! Oh, I *suspected* something was up. Suddenly you couldn't stand her." Rosanna slammed a can of beans on the counter, and he flinched. "You kept talking about how ostentatious she was. I asked you about it, and you fucking lied to me. You even had the audacity to roll your eyes."

"It was over by then. It was just once. I didn't want you getting hurt."

"Do you have any conscience at all, Osin? Do you have any feelings?"

"Oh, Rosie, I was younger then. I've changed. Look, I didn't cheat on Merrill." He tapped his chest. "I was the one who got screwed."

"So when did this happen?" She waited. "Tell me, goddamn it!"

"It was so long ago I don't remember. Maybe a year before I moved out. It was only once."

"No, no, it couldn't be. She had moved to Seattle by then." She was rubbing the counter in a threateningly out-of-control way. Her hands were flushed. "Wait—we took that camping trip. Tell me it wasn't then."

When she raised her hand, Osin thought she was going to smack him. But instead she started crying, a high-pitched raggedy sound, like cloth tearing. It was the distressing soundtrack of the divorce.

"Oh, Rosie, please. Don't get upset."

She was bent over awkwardly, her elbows on the counter. Good sense told him not to approach. He thought of her standing in the driveway twenty years ago, yelling something about a dry pot roast. Her hair was knotty, she was wearing his coat, for some reason. Her legs were bare. The police came, and she'd continued to scream, calling him a cunt-loving whore. He hadn't been aware she knew those words.

She raised her bloated face now and looked at him. "You're an asshole, Osin. So selfish."

"Come on, Rosie. Please. I'm sorry."

"And I let you stay. Me. I let you stay in my house, so you could use me again. So you could walk all over me like you used to."

"That's not true. Why are you saying that? That's not true."

"Boy, I must be really screwed up. This whole time I thought I was doing something good by helping you. That's a laugh. You don't deserve it! You just shit on the people who help you!"

"What?" This conversation was gathering the terrible speed of a nightmare. "That's not true!"

"I'm just enabling the same garbage I did with my own father. Forty years later and I'm still doing it. All that mental trash! It has nothing to do with you at all! You're just the way I'm able make myself feel bad."

"How can you say that? That's not—"

"You're so awful," she said. "You're so awful to me."

She was sobbing over the counter. He wanted to touch her, but he didn't have the nerve. "I think you just need a little time to calm down, " he said. He let himself out of the house.

III

That night he slept in his own bedroom in Marin. He woke up, sweaty and disoriented, thinking he was in the basement at Rosanna's, before they converted it into a playroom for Richard. Rosanna had gotten the contractor quotes, arranged for the electrician, gone over the plans, and was home every day supervising the work. Yet Osin complained bitterly when he saw that some caulk had gotten on the window. He never apologized for that. How could she compare him to her father, that tough, heavily lined man sitting in a wingback chair, sipping a scotch and soda. A drinker. He had an erratic cruelty. Joking with you and then suddenly a chill would come into the conversation, and he'd cut you with an insult. You'd look up and he wouldn't be smiling. Call you a "dummy" mostly, or a "do nothing." He was smart and had a dry sort of humor—when he was sober. He wasn't all bad—he gave them the down payment on the house, called Rosie "his little girl." She hadn't exactly cowered in his presence. She used to tease him even, about his weight, or the farm he kept saying he wanted to buy someday. He'd been dead now for decades.

Osin reached over to the bedside phone and dialed Rosanna's number. He got the machine. "Listen. Rosie. You're right. I was completely in the wrong. But it was so many years ago. I feel awful about it now. If you never want to speak to me again I'll understand." Best to leave this whole business with her father out of it. She was just upset, didn't know what she was saying. "I'm going through withdrawal from your tea. You can't leave me in this state." He affected a chuckle. "Call me. It's Osin."

He assumed, when the phone rang five minutes later, that it was her, but it turned out to be a digital satellite salesperson. Twice he went to call her again, but made himself hold off. He stayed inside; his house had the diminished presence of a former bully. Standing in the living room, he felt distracted and slightly bored—a houseguest in his own home, separated from all of his amusements. He wandered into the kitchen and looked out the window. It was a warm day, and he considered doing some yard work, but the gardeners had already come.

Finally, at around eight-thirty that night, when Rosanna would be getting ready to watch Masterpiece Theater, he called again. She didn't pick up. "Rosanna, it's me. Osin. I know you're usually home at this time." He waited respectfully for a few seconds. Nothing. He sighed into the receiver. "Is what I did really so terrible?" He paused. "Yes, yes it is. But I don't know what to say besides I'm sorry. Please answer." He waited. Then he hung up. He spent the rest of the evening in front of the TV set, drinking scotch and eating stale crackers.

Two days went by and he wasn't even sure how they'd been spent. He had regressed into his old habits, the habits of a spaniel, waiting for the mail, looking out the window. Sometimes he didn't dress until mid afternoon. The first day he'd tried going for a walk down his block. But most of the time he spent indoors, puttering around, or thinking about the past.

Many times it was Richard as a boy, sitting at the kitchen table, clenching his pencil, trying to figure out a math problem. Osin saying, "Don't press down so hard.

You'll tear the paper." Rosanna, her face moist from the steam over the stove. "I can't believe the fondue came out, but it did! You have to try it. I'm a genius." The way the light took the trees in the evening behind the house. Merrill in the tub, asking him to soap her back. He was waiting for Richard in the darkening park. "One more ball dad, please?" The kid was throwing them up and swinging at them himself, while Osin stood on the edge of the field in his suit and tie. "Let's go, Ritchie." Impatient. So impatient. He couldn't relax. Where did he have to go anyway? What could have been so important?

He was still thinking useless thoughts, except now he went backwards instead of forwards. Nothing had changed. He had been distracted, short-sighted, a chaser of butterflies. He had fled from one home to another.

What if Rosanna was done with him for good? The thought was enough to send him into a mild panic. He called her again and when she didn't pick up, he drove to the florist. Recognizing the salesgirl, he was so grateful to see a familiar face, he started blabbering. "Seems like I'm in the doghouse again! Let's see how I get myself out."

She smiled and opened the cooler. "For your wife?"

"Yes," he said, stumbling through the slip. "But she hates roses. Nothing too high-end. She likes bouquet filler, weeds. Hell, I should just go to the Rt. 101 median and clip them myself."

She laughed. Her pert face tipped up towards him, as if to be kissed. There was a time when he had wanted to sleep with this girl too. Now all he felt was mild irritation. "Irises are too fancy," he said. "Here—give me some of these fluffy things."

Afterwards he stopped by the liquor store and picked up a bottle of Crème de Menthe, the liquor Rosanna favored.

She'd take one sip from the mini fluted glass and pour the rest over her ice cream.

When he got to her house, he saw that her car was missing. He was standing in the driveway wondering where she was, when the fat man across the street called out, "She left about an hour ago."

"You know, you probably shouldn't tell strangers that." He disliked this neighbor, who had a moist handshake and called Rosanna a "great gal" enough times to make Osin worry there was an obsessive edge to the admiration.

The man gave his hedges a quick spray with the hose. His socks were pulled up to mid-calf. Osin turned back to the car and the neighbor, whose name was possibly Jim, shouted, "Well, you're here often enough, so I figure you're safe. We look out for each other on this block."

"The neighborhood watch thing. Terrific."

"I keep a special eye out for Rosanna. Make sure she's not being bothered."

Was this a threat? Jim had moved to the side of the house and was now hosing down the siding.

"Well, I have some work to do here," Osin said. The man didn't reply, and Osin went around to the back stoop. An hour went by. He expected Jim to come around and check his story.

Osin was urinating on the maple tree when Rosanna finally showed up. It was after two. Strangely nervous, he zipped up his fly and ran to grab the presents off the stoop.

She spotted him as she was getting out of the car. "I don't want to talk to you, Osin."

He darted an eye over to the neighbor's house, but all was quiet. "Please, just listen! I've come all the way out here."

She snorted. "All the way out here." She looked down at his hands, which offered the gifts. "Flowers! We've sunk to a whole new level of absurdity now." She took the bottle of liqueur tied with a ribbon. "I haven't had this stuff in years."

"I'm very sorry, Rosie."

She turned hard. Apologizing to a woman often had that effect. "I haven't forgiven you," she said. "In fact I've started to reevaluate how I think of you."

"Reevaluate! This happened twenty years ago. Isn't the person who's been sitting around with you for the past week more important?"

"I'm not sure I like that person either."

"I thought we were getting along." Was he able to assess anything accurately? Merrill had been unhappy enough to cheat. Rosanna pretended to enjoy his company when she didn't. At least he knew where he stood with Richard. He knew Richard disliked him.

"You said some pretty cruel things too," he reminded her.

"Were they? Or were they just honest?"

"You know I'm not really in the mood to be abused. I just came over to apologize. Nothing more. So enjoy your liquor and your flowers." He started to walk over to his car.

She said, "You always do this—you always turn it around on me when you are clearly in the wrong."

"I know I'm in the wrong! That's what I'm saying. I've had a revelation about my life and the way—"

"A revelation." She sounded disgusted.

He had been prepared to spill out the contents of the past few days. The images of Richard, of Rosanna in her scarf, his sense of waste. But instead, he got annoyed. "You always put me down. It must make you feel pretty good that I turned out as shitty as you predicted. I bet the only reason you let me back in was so you could have a good laugh."

"No one's laughing. The whole situation is pathetic and sad. I can't even keep the pleasant memories of our marriage because you always seem to find a way to undercut them. Now I'm both alone and a fool."

"You have fond memories of our marriage?"

She looked at him as if he were crazy. "Of course I do. You gave me our son."

That was the one thing he could never figure out, a split-second, a spasm, that years of negligence were unable to overturn. "I've enjoyed being with you this last few weeks," he said. "It hasn't all been escapism and fear."

"I know."

"I feel at ease with you. At peace. But you're right—this type of arrangement couldn't go on forever. Eventually, I had to face the reality of my house. Of my life."

"This is reality, too, I guess. Us standing here right now." She sounded as if she were forgiving him, and Osin resisted the urge to look at her for confirmation. Instead, he looked up. The sky was a gingery color, streaked with clouds. A beautiful evening.

He let Asmarina go. He couldn't afford the chance that Rosanna would walk in and realize she'd been deceived again. Or even worse, think Osin had brought back another woman to reenact the past. He was spending less time at Rosanna's, but he kept up his end of the housework and discovered his meticulous nature was fulfilled.

Rosanna saw him mopping the kitchen. "Oh, I guess I'll do the living room then."

"I just did the living room."

"It's filthy. I felt the grit on my feet when I just walked through."

"I vacuumed," he said. "Maybe I missed that part."

"Don't take offense, but I've noticed things have

gone downhill. I assumed you thought you could slack off now that you weren't here all the time."

Part of the reason he hadn't been here that frequently was he sensed Rosanna was avoiding him. She was eating her breakfast before he got up, then she spent most of the day out and read in her room after dinner. Fed up, he walked in there one night and accused, "Why are you ignoring me!"

"Jesus, Osin! I thought you went home. Don't you knock?" She was sitting up in bed, in her nightgown, a patchwork quilt over her legs. Her face looked shiny.

"If you have something on your mind, you should discuss it."

"I don't have anything on my mind. Perhaps it's your guilty conscience."

"Well if you have nothing against me why don't we sit downstairs and have coffee. I've already brewed it."

"It's almost ten o'clock! I'm not having coffee now."

He ran his fingers over the maple dresser, which was dusty. He used to keep his cufflinks and change there, in a narrow monogrammed tray next to the lamp.

"I can't believe you still sleep in our old bed," he said. "I would have thought you'd be more superstitious."

Rosanna took off her reading glasses and put them on the table next to the tissues and cold cream. A stack of magazines was on the floor. *Family Circle. Modern Maturity.* The smiling man on the cover had teeth that appeared wolfish and artificial.

He tried again. "It's not good to keep these things bottled up."

The dresser's top drawer was ajar, and Osin nudged it open with his index finger. Women's undergarments always had the power to excite him, ever since he was a boy. Rosanna's were the full-seated kind. Cotton. Although here was a satin pair with big, blotchy flowers.

He rubbed it between his thumb and forefinger. Nothing stirring in the lower regions.

"Osin! Get your damn hands out of there."

"Come on, Rosanna. Talk. I can take it."

She hesitated. "Well, if you must know, I keep picturing you and Susan together."

"Do you picture it with the way I looked then, or right now?"

"What? *Then.* You had that awful handlebar mustache. Ugh—" She turned her head away. "It makes me sick just thinking about it. I looked at that picture again before I took it down and destroyed it."

He had noticed the photo had been replaced by a recent shot of her and Richard. "What I wanted was to hear more about those things you said about your father. How I'm like him."

"What do you want to know?"

"How you could think that! I'm not like him. I don't drink like him for one. I'm much thinner. My table manners are better. I don't call people 'dirty idiots'..."

"Well, it's not a one-to-one comparison. I did notice some similarities when we got married. Your sense of humor. It's more about my desire to seek approval from you, when a lot of times you don't treat me so well. I can be a little mealy-mouthed."

"I don't think you're mealy-mouthed at all! You order me around."

"Reacting isn't the same as acting."

He took a breath and exhaled slowly. "So what do you want to do?"

"I didn't realize there was a decision to be made here. Would you like me to kick you out?"

He resisted the urge to come over to the bed and stretch out next to her. Instead he tapped his knuckle against the dresser. "I thought I had been doing you some good."

She sighed. "We've known each other a long time. Even the fact that we still communicate counts for something."

IV

Osin had noticed that Richard called his mother every weekday afternoon at around two. "He's still tied tightly to those apron strings, isn't he?" Osin said to Rosanna.

"Maybe he has abandonment issues."

"It's you he keeps checking in on. What does that say?"

When the phone rang at two-fifteen, Osin quickly picked it up.

"You're answering the phone now?" Richard said. Through the wires, his voice was a register deeper.

"I hear an officious beeping—you must be at your desk. So, any big placements today? Or is it a slow time of year? I was reading in the papers that the job market is looking up for high-end tech jobs."

"Is Mom there?"

Osin watched Rosanna walk upstairs. "She's in the bathroom. Do you want me to take a message for you?"

Richard sighed. "It's not that important. I wanted to see if she still had the old Lionel train set."

"My set?"

"Oh, I thought it was her father's. Forget it, then."

"I think it may be up in the attic somewhere," Osin said. "I remember taking it down and packing—"

"Don't worry about it. You don't know where anything is. We moved all the boxes around last winter."

"I'll give it a look anyway. What the hell. Listen, I was thinking, maybe now we have the time, we can go to a ball game or something. Take along Bernard."

"I'm busy."

"Busy! Your mother said you're not even putting in forty hours over there."

"Just tell Mom I called, okay?" Richard said.

The trapdoor to the attic was in Rosanna's bedroom closet. She stopped him as he was cutting through. "What are you doing?"

"Richard called."

"And?"

"It's our business. He wanted me to help him find something." Osin shoved aside a row of hangers, exposing the ladder rungs nailed to the wall.

"Careful of my dresses," Rosanna called after him.

Up in the musty attic, Osin saw that nothing had been rearranged. You could hardly move up here. Boxes were piled on top of one another, all within arm's distance of the trapdoor. It was a wonder the weight didn't bring the ceiling down.

One squirrel-nibbled box was labeled with his name. The train couldn't be that easy to find. It turned out to contain china from his mother's house. After ten minutes of searching, he was about to give up; dust motes flew around in the air, and it was becoming difficult to breath. He dug out another box with his name on it. Instead, it was packed with Rosanna's old books—an entire box on parenting. She had been so anxious to have Richard. *Baby's First Year. Name Your Baby. Getting Your Child Through Divorce.* He picked that one up. The cover was yellowed. He flipped through the seventies line drawings, turning to the chapter on adult children: "Be prepared for resentments that may not surface until years later." He carefully climbed down the ladder and went to find Rosanna.

"This describes Richard to a T," he said, holding out the splayed book.

"Where'd you find this? It's disintegrating."

"The attic. Look—*sullen, bitter, curt*. It says that some children, especially those eager to please, won't have the courage to express their discontent or anxiety at the time of the divorce. Instead they let it fester. So, it was both of our faults." He tapped the page. "Ritchie and I got along great up until seven years ago and then—Bam!"

"How can you possibly think things were great? He didn't want you to come to his high school graduation."

"Spats. The high school one was over joining the football team. I had objected, remember? And I still went to the ceremony. Listen to this, 'to heal relationships with adult children, you have to excavate the lies of their childhood'." Osin closed the book. "I need to take this situation by the horns. The boy and I don't have all the time in the world. He's coming over this afternoon, isn't he?"

"Listen, try and use a little diplomacy, okay? You get such bad results when you rush at things head on."

Osin was waiting on the porch when Richard drove up. "Hey!" he said, waving. He strode over to the Bronco. Why did the kid need such a big vehicle, like a construction worker? "I was wondering when you'd show."

Richard was wearing oversized aviator sunglasses. Maybe this was another symptom of repressed pain, hiding your eyes behind dark glasses all the time.

Richard rolled down the window only halfway. "You're still here?"

Osin addressed Bernard, who was sitting in the back, his hair slicked down in a wide part. "You're looking spiffy. Where's your girlfriend?"

"Uh," he said. "School. I hate girls."

"School? You mean daycare?"

Richard interrupted, "No, he means school. Preschool."

"They start you early with your sums and letters, don't they?" Osin said, unbuckling Bernard from the seat. With this much advance preparation the kid could be a physicist. Bernard's t-shirt was damp to the touch. Osin put him down on the lawn. "Listen, your dad and I need to have a talk. Run along inside. Granny's waiting in there with ice cream." A white lie—Osin had finished the last of the Breyer's that morning. Rosanna would come up with something.

He watched Bernard sprint up to the house. "He's a charmer," he said to Richard. "Good attitude."

Richard, who was bent into the cargo area, said nothing. He had developed broad-shoulders, which gave him a blue-collar look. Osin had been wrong to worry he would stay frail-looking his whole life.

"So what's on the agenda for today?" Osin asked.

"I'm going to empty the gutters. Then I have to take a look at the bathroom faucet upstairs that's dripping."

It was rather humiliating that even with him here, Richard still had to drive over and handle the upkeep. "Well, I'm sure I can be of some assistance."

Richard looked as if he doubted this.

For the gutters, Richard was the one who got up on the aluminum ladder, while Osin stayed below, embracing the trash barrel. From above Richard threw down clumps of rotten, foul-smelling leaves, occasionally hitting Osin in the arm. The smell was like the interior of a decaying mouth.

After several minutes Osin realized the boy intended to work in silence the entire time, as if the barrel were just sitting on the ground. "There are some things I need to get off my chest," Osin called up. "There's something that's been bothering me for a long time."

Richard, cut out against the cloudless sky, looked imposing, like a giant. "The divorce?"

"No, no, farther back." To his own ears, his voice sounded hollow. His pulse was racing. "When your mother was pregnant with you, we took a cruise. She gets seasick very easily and was throwing up the whole time. We were miserable. We couldn't even sit through dinner. I said, 'Why don't you take these pills?'" Osin felt the burning shame. Had he ever before, thinking about it? Or is it that once we identify the negative impact of past actions, we can no longer get by as innocents. "She didn't want to. I kept pressuring her. Bullying, even, until she did."

"So what?"

"Well, I think it led to your difficulties with reading."

The clumps of leaves stopped falling. "I did well in school. In college I was on the dean's list for two years."

"You were able to overcome it." Osin nodded. "You were a very hardworking kid. Very hardworking." He wondered if he should tell Richard how low his IQ was.

"I can't believe this is what you choose to focus on instead of the divorce."

"Yeah, well, I don't understand the whole divorce thing. It never seemed to bother you back then." Osin was tempted to disparage Judy, but decided against it. "We still went out and did things together, Ritchie. It's not like I moved across the continent. Look at your friend, the Thompson kid. His old man used to beat the living crap out of him. You could have been that kid. He had something to gripe about."

"Jesus, nice example."

"You and I did things together. We were buddies. Remember I took you to Candlestick Park. And then all of a sudden twenty years later, you're upset."

"I was miserable that day."

"The day we went to the game?" Osin remembered the air from the ocean, the roaring of the crowd, and his young son beside him, standing up when the ball was hit. "It was a great time."

"I hated every minute of it." Richard kept his back to Osin, so that it seemed he was speaking to someone on the roof. "I had to sit there and pretend I didn't know about your affairs. Like you and I were betraying Mom together. You kept pushing hotdogs on me."

"You ordered those hotdogs." Osin remembered the boy's pale face bent over the enormous cup of HI-C, mournfully sipping. Like now, he had refused to make eye contact. "I thought you had fun. I don't know what to say."

Up above Richard's hands were shaking, making the sun flicker. "You never do. And now that things have gotten rough, you move back in here to suck off Mom!"

"I'm not sucking off her!" said Osin. "I give her money."

"Taking advantage like you always do. She probably listens to your self-involved bullshit."

This hurt. "We have our own arrangement. She enjoys my company. Ask her. Ask her yourself."

"Just let me do the gutters, okay, and then I'll be out of here."

"No, Ritchie. If you're upset with me, we should discuss—"

Richard turned around, his face inflamed. "Go! I mean it. Or I'll say things I shouldn't."

From the window Osin watched Richard leave, kissing Bernard on the head before buckling him into the car seat. Osin felt wiped out from the assault, like he needed to go lie down. Passing by the open bathroom door, he saw Rosanna down on her knees, replacing a knob on the toilet base. She pointed up at him.

Osin said, "I don't want to talk about it."

"Why? What happened?"

"I screwed it up. You were right—I should never have been a father."

"I never said that."

"Yes, you did. Right after the divorce."

"Oh." She patted the handkerchief around her hair. "You have a very selective memory. I'm sure I said a lot of things."

"Well, he hates me now. He also said I'm living off you. Sucking off you." "You are."

"What? No, I'm not! Who collected the fat alimony checks, here?"

"All right." She stood up. "Let's not get ugly. Richard's just protective of me, that's all."

"Maybe you are helping me out by letting me stay." He hadn't realized his needs were so transparent. Even the boy could see it. "But you're getting my company too, you know. You looked pretty bored before I came around."

"I don't think 'bored' is quite the right word. Tranquil." She smiled. When Osin turned to leave, she said, "Don't worry too much about Richard. He'll come around."

But Richard was stubborn. He remembered his round-faced son at four years old explaining, in great detail, that people only existed while in his presence. The boy had called Mrs. Murphy a liar when she said she'd just been to the dentist before picking him up.

"If I didn't know you better," he said to Rosanna, "I'd think you'd poisoned him against me."

That night, unable to sleep, Osin called Merrill. Twisting the sheets in his hand, he waited for her to answer. She had always sided with him about Richard. She had said Richard was selfish and stubborn. Her own family had been horrendous, a bunch of alcoholics who threatened each other with shotguns late at night. The phone rang emptily into the other side.

As much as Osin tried to put Richard out of his head, he kept replaying the scene by the house. How had Ritchie known about the affairs? He and Rosanna should have been more careful, hollering in the heat of anger. The kid was sensitive. Richard would force himself to eavesdrop on the fights even if it killed him, just so he could be prepared for the worst. His son was right; Osin was a poor parent—his own father would have been ashamed.

"I was stupid to think this problem would go away on its own," he told Rosanna the next afternoon. "I need to hold a family meeting."

"I suggest you call it something else," she said. "The term could be incendiary."

"However you want to spin it. You're the one doing the inviting."

"What's this about?"

"It's a surprise."

Rosanna started to go upstairs. "You're crazy if you think I'm going to have them over here with an undisclosed agenda."

Osin sighed. "All right. It's about my will."

"Are you cutting them out?"

"No. Stop asking so many questions. And who's 'they'? I'm not giving Judy anything." Osin rifled through the sideboard drawer looking for a notepad. "Make sure Bernard shows. It's important that he be here."

Rosanna was able to assemble them for Wednesday night. Osin put on a sports coat and even shined his shoes. He shouldn't have bothered. Both Judy and Richard showed up in their yard work clothes. From the stairway, Osin watched Ritchie walk in. His shoulders were hunched like a resentful teenager's.

Once they were settled, Osin stepped in front of the fireplace with the manila folder of paperwork he'd requested from his lawyer. He'd also, as a last minute idea, picked up several investment brochures from Wells Fargo, in case Ritchie wanted to look through them. He beamed at the group. "First, I want to thank—"

Richard cut him off. "Okay, so what's this about?"

"I'm changing my will." Osin let his eyes linger on each face. "It will benefit everyone in this room."

"What were the terms before? Had you cut us out?"

It occurred to Osin that his son had interpreted the flare-up from the other day as a license to be openly rude. "No, of course not. But the executor changed and some other things were altered."

"I see." Richard leaned back in his chair. "You're doing this before your own divorce, so that Merrill can't contest her share."

Osin was about to reply when Rosanna cut him off. "Richard! Let your father speak."

He was surprised to see how seriously the boy took the reprimand. Ritchie frowned at the floor.

"I expected some hostility," said Osin. "I know I haven't been perfect. But I'm doing this for Bernard. I'm establishing a trust fund. It's what my father would have done for you, Ritchie, if he'd had the dough." Instead the old man had set up a Super Savings account, as Osin remembered, and deposited ten dollars in there for each major holiday. Richard had spent the money on movies and sports equipment the summer after his high school graduation.

Judy, always the calculating one, said, "How much are we talking about here? And more importantly, are there any strings attached?"

"No," Osin said. "Of course there aren't. Although I would like it if the boy went to a decent college. It should be enough for tuition." Bernard seemed like a sharp kid, but he was also a little happy-go-lucky. If he didn't turn out to be college material, let him start up a business. Osin turned to Bernard, "There might even be enough for your own pony."

"A pony!" said Bernard.

Judy said swiftly, "Your grandfather was talking about a stuffed pony, like Bill." To Osin, she said, "How do we know you're not going to change your mind again?"

"It's locked in. Jesus. I don't know what you're so concerned about. Your father's the one with the shipyard money. I'm surprised he hasn't offered something similar." Back on the East Coast, that tightwad was sitting on a pile of coins that rivaled a celebrity's.

"How do you know he hasn't?" Judy thrust her freckled chin at him, angling for an argument. What it must be like to live with her on a daily basis.

"Well, anyway," Osin said, "the fund wouldn't be affected even if I were to remarry, or have another child." Rosanna snorted, and Osin addressed Richard. "The other major change is that I would like you to be the executor of my will, Ritchie."

His son looked up suspiciously. "Why?"

"Because you're my only son, damn it! I'm trying to do something nice. It isn't easy to contemplate my own death, you know."

"I'm sure you'll last for many more years," Rosanna said, getting up. "Richard, tell him you'll be the executor of the will. It means something to him, even though his manner is crass."

"Crass!" said Osin. "I dressed up for this fucking occasion."

"Osin!" Judy said. "Watch your language. Bernard's right there." His grandson, after fishing around in Osin's pockets, had run over to his mother.

"All right," Richard said. "Fine." His big half-tint glasses were already focused on the door. "Thank you, I guess." Again, he didn't look Osin in the face.

After they all left, Rosanna said, "That was a very nice thing you did with the trust fund."

"Yeah, yeah." Osin slumped down on the couch. He didn't even get the chance to crack his folder to show Richard the new terms. "Ungrateful son of a bitch."

"Osin!"

"You always stick up for him—against me."

"That's because you're usually in the wrong. You need to be patient. You can't just throw some money at him and expect him to be—"

"Hey, I came in there with very low expectations. The lowest. Would it kill him to be gracious?"

Osin's cell phone rang. "Who the hell is this?" He looked. It was Merrill.

Immediately, his hands started shaking. He opened the phone. "Hello?" he said, striding towards the stairs and up to the safety of his study.

"Osin. It's me."

"Yes." The blood beat in his ears. He closed the door. "I'm surprised to hear from you. And at—" he looked at the clock, ten p.m.—"this late. Where are you?"

"I'm at my house." She sounded peevish. "Eric's. Why do you always ask me that?"

He suppressed the urge to ask where Eric was. "Is everything all right?"

"Of course." She hesitated. "No. I don't know. I don't know why I'm calling."

Osin felt the adrenaline go to his knees.

"I was just thinking about you," said Merrill. He heard a drawer shut. Where was she? In the kitchen? "I was just cleaning out some of my boxes and ran into the old Bermuda brochures. Remember I got sun poisoning on that trip? You panicked. Running down to the front desk every two minutes." Her voice went deeper to mimic his. "'Get a doctor, you idiot! My wife's in pain!' You screamed so much I think that poor girl quit after we left."

Osin chuckled cautiously. Was she drunk? He wasn't sure if he should join in.

"This isn't easy. Nothing turned out the way it was supposed to."

"I know," he agreed.

This was evidently the wrong thing to say, because she blurted, "I shouldn't have called." She hesitated, and Osin could hear her breathing into the receiver. "It's just that I miss you."

"I miss you too, Merrill." This must be true, but yet he felt blank when he said it.

Her voice went down a pitch. "Why did you call me the other night and not leave a message? What were you going to say?"

"Oh, I don't know. Nothing probably." With his thumb, he circled a water stained ring on the desk. "I just wanted to speak with you. Why didn't you pick up?"

"Eric was there."

Osin stiffened. "What about those other times, then? When I left you that letter. Why are you just getting around to calling me now?"

"Why are you yelling?"

"I'm not! I'm trying to—"

In a rough voice, she said, "I didn't call to fight. This was a bad idea. I regret it already. Take care of yourself, all right?"

Osin was left holding the dead phone to his ear.

By mid afternoon the next day he was still thinking about Merrill's sudden confession. What if she really was interested in reuniting with him? The thought made him go light with anxiety. The timing couldn't be worse with the announcement of the will. Would he even be able to change it back? Richard had appeared not to care, but he'd exploit the issue.

Outside Osin's bedroom door, partially blocking the exit, Rosanna had left several cardboard boxes with a note: *Some of your things. Please sort through when you have "time."* He was about to step over them when he saw a box labeled "Boat." He pulled it open right there in the hallway. Inside were old plans for a rowboat he had wanted to build. Holding the crumbling paper, he went to find Rosanna. She was outside, digging around the rose bushes.

He called out, "Remember how Sig Murphy had that rowboat he'd built. We used to take it down to the inlets off Half Moon Bay and fish."

She looked up from underneath a large floppy sunhat. "Not really."

"Don't you remember how he gave me the plans for it so that I could build one? It was all I could talk about for months."

"How many years ago was this? You never built it, obviously."

"No, but look what I found!" He spread the blueprints on the grass in front of her. He'd been obsessed with that boat.

Rosanna pressed the papers down with her fingertips. "Building a rowboat seems a really hard thing to do."

Seeing her bent over in that ridiculously big hat, Osin felt uncomfortably guilty. He should tell her he spoke to Merrill, but he wasn't sure how to frame it.

"You don't have any experience with boats," Rosanna continued. "It needs to be watertight. The wood has to be treated so it bends."

"Sig did it. He didn't have any experience." Osin rolled up the plans. "You're the one who's always telling me to get a hobby and now look. The naysayer."

She started laughing.

"What?"

"I was just picturing you out on this boat that you'd made yourself. It sinking down in a little pathetic circle—" she swirled her finger—"like a toy."

"First thing's first," Osin said. "I need to assess my tool situation. Where are my tools?"

"What tools?"

"The ones I left here when I moved."

"The garage, maybe?" She got up. "You're really throwing yourself into this, aren't you?"

Deep in the familiar leaf mold smell of the garage, he found them. Rosanna had his entire life boxed up and secreted away all over this house. Even his own mother hadn't bothered to keep so many of his things.

He nudged the box with his toe; it had give. Inside the tools were jumbled together, their blades facing each other. There was an orange electrical cord wrapped around the saw. "Nothing is sorted."

"Well then sort it. They're your things."

He felt a sudden flush of generosity. "I'll do you one better. I'll put the boat on hold. First, I'm going to build you a tool bench."

"I could care less about a tool bench. Build me something else. A potting shed."

"I'll put a section in for your gardening things. I can—" His phone jangled. He slid it out of his pocket—Merrill. Automatically, his heart started thumping.

"You're certainly popular," said Rosanna. "Who is it?"

"Merrill," he told her, opening the phone. Her jaw dropped as he turned his back on her, shielding the phone with his body. "Hello?" he said.

"Why do you answer like that when you know it's me?" Merrill said. He heard a rushing sound and guessed she was driving. "How are you?"

Rosanna strode out to the garden. Her wide, angry back condemned him. Osin walked over to the maple, stood underneath, absentmindedly rubbed the bark.

"I was at the organic market today and almost bought your brand of waffles, without thinking," Merrill said. "It's funny how habits are hard to break. The grain ones, remember?"

"Yeah," said Osin. Why was she telling him this? "I do like those."

"Have you been eating them? I remember leaving two boxes in the freezer." Osin realized with a start that she thought he was at the house. Where was she, in the car? He was having difficulty picturing her face. All he could see were her slim, white fingers gripping the wheel, the phone headset, the beanbag frog she kept on the dash.

"Listen," she said, "I feel bad about the way we left things yesterday."

He sighed. "Don't worry about it." Really, he was going to pay for this with Rosanna. He probably shouldn't have picked up with her standing there.

"I just don't like all this tension. It felt like you were accusing me again."

"That's not what I was trying to do. Maybe we should meet, instead of all this phoning. We could have coffee."

"No. That's not a good idea."

Annoyed, he said, "Well, why do you keep calling then?"

"I've missed you." Her voice was heavy with nostalgia. How could she just call up to announce a desire she had no intention of following up on. He'd forgotten this about her, that she had very little self-control. It was probably what led her into the affair in the first place.

"Trouble with Eric in the love shack?" he asked.

"Do you want me to discuss this with you?"

"No. I don't."

But Merrill plowed ahead anyway. "He talks so much. He thinks he knows everything. He is very smart, but still."

Osin decided to ignore this. Eric had thought Pol Pot was Vietnamese, which explained the vague and confused political discussion Osin tried to have with him once. Eric had brought up the topic. "He didn't have a whole hell of a lot to say when I met him," Osin said. "Plus, he's got that stutter."

"He almost never does that. It was just that one time. He was nervous."

It occurred to Osin why. "It was disgusting the way he was spitting on himself."

"It's more that his conversations jump all over the place. He always has to dominate. It's like he talks at me. I guess I knew this, but it's different when you live with the person."

"This is true." He thought about what a hard adjustment it had been when he first married Merrill, having to constantly field seemingly paranoid questions about his inner moods.

"So I'm having a rough time," she said in a deepened voice of confidentiality. "Quite frankly, it's causing me to question some of the decisions I made."

"That's not surprising," Osin said. Again he felt the heaviness in his chest.

"I have to go. I just pulled up to the open house. I'll call you later."

He suspected that this phone call was just a means of getting back at Eric. Surely she must recognize Osin stripped of his earning power, with his neuroses, and his stray old man body hair. Just talking to her was exhausting. What would seeing her do, being with her again? Even before their separation, Merrill was lit up in a sexual frenzy. She had prompted Osin to go see his doctor, as if his lack of ability was unnatural. The thought of attempting to have sex with Merrill every night was vaguely frightening.

When he went into the kitchen, later, to get himself a snack, Rosanna was there. She glared at him from the stove, banging pots. They couldn't talk freely; her ally was over again, doing something underneath the sink. The place seemed to require constant fixing, or maybe Richard used it as an excuse to get away from Judy. Osin didn't say hello. He and his son were barely speaking to each other. Osin had forgiven him for the will incident, but his son was still carrying the grudge.

Osin had bought a woodworking magazine at the store, and he brought it over to the kitchen table so that he could overhear anything that was said about him.

It was just starting to dawn on him how little he knew about construction. He would probably need to plane the wood first. Or could he get it already planed? He flipped through the magazine. It didn't give a definite answer. His father, the reddened old worker, had built a whole house with his own beefy hands. Where had Osin been? Inside with his mother somewhere, and baby brother Willie, playing with model trains and dreaming.

Once Rosanna had left the kitchen, Osin said, "You know how to build?"

Richard, still kneeling by the sink, said, "yes," in a way that sounded like "no."

Osin brought over the magazine, pointing to the glossy photo. "All right. Explain to me how to cut the cornicing here."

"I'm in the middle of something."

"When you have time, then." Osin went back to the table. "I can wait."

As he suspected, Richard's reluctance was mostly show. He came over and looked down at Osin's hand-written notes. "You should start by hashing out the basic structure first. Taking down the dimensions."

"Eight feet by—"

"Is this a free standing structure?" Richard asked.

Osin hadn't decided. "Here, let's go out to the garage and I'll show you."

They went out, his son lumbering beside him. Osin pointed to the free space of wall, then the tools.

"You're using all hand tools for this job? You've got to be kidding me." Richard picked up the plane. "This blade isn't even sharp."

"What do you want? Those are your mother's things. That man with the twitch, the one who lives two houses down, he borrowed the hammer and never returned it. I'll probably have to buy a new one." Osin dug through the box.

"Well, I can bring over some stuff," Richard said. "But it would be easier if you had a standing band saw for this."

Osin wrote down "band saw" on a little pad. "Best to put the money in the equipment now. I'll bend to your lead." Out of the corner of his eye, he could see his son softening with the compliment. Richard had gotten out a measuring tape and was marking off the wall. "Tell me what I need and where to get it," said Osin.

That evening Osin brought his gin and tonic into the living room. He was damned if he was going to let Rosanna intimidate him. Merrill was still legally his wife. He picked up the newest issue of *Modern Maturity*. So many pharmaceutical ads—a bad sign. He was reading an article on heartburn when Rosanna came swishing by. She was in a beige silk garment that was too dressy to be a nightgown.

"What are you trying on clothes for?" he asked.

"I have a date."

"A *date*?"

"Yes, Osin." She went over to the cabineted lowboy and started rustling around in the papers and junk.

"How long have you been plotting this?"

"Plotting! You should talk."

He ignored the jab. "Well, I had planned on barbecuing pork chops tonight," he said. "But I guess you're entitled to go out, if you really feel the need." He shrugged. "I need to do work on your potting bench, anyway."

"The neighbors don't want to hear you banging around out there in the middle of the night. And—" she hesitated "—I'd prefer to have the house to myself."

"Why?"

"Osin. Come on. You should spend the night at your house, anyway. When was the last time you were back there? I've seen you in that same pair of pants for at least a week. The place could have burned down by now."

"No. The landscapers would have told me."

"You have an hour."

Should he argue her down? But he didn't want to get into a lengthy discussion about Merrill. When he thought about her, all he felt was a faint buzzing. The phone had been silent all evening, tucked away into his back pocket. He checked it every few minutes.

He followed Rosanna into the bathroom and stood in the doorway as she applied her makeup—what women do to disguise reality. "You know," he said, "the Elizabethans called makeup 'paint'. Even the syphilitics would slap on the powder while the skin crumbled beneath their fingers."

Rosanna, ignoring him, used a foam pad to apply cream to her eyelids.

"Don't you think you're getting a little long in the tooth to go running around town?" he said.

She dropped the corner of one lid and stretched the other. "No."

"We're practically the same age!"

"And yet I seem years younger." She blinked at herself in the mirror and picked up a wide brush. "Everyone always said that when looking at the two of us. It's attitude." She dropped the brush and it clattered against the sink. "I would advise you to go out and get a date too, but then again you're still married. You have Merrill's feelings to consider."

"Merrill and I are separated! Where have you been?"

She was dusting a pinkish hue onto her cheeks, unconvinced. How he'd ever managed to fool her on the other affairs was beyond him.

"I'm not here to judge," she said in a judgmental tone. "But it's getting time you moved on with your life." She turned her mismatched eyes on him. "You can't stay here forever."

"Is that a threat?" he asked.

"No. It's reality." As she brushed past him, he smelled tea rose, her special occasion perfume.

She insisted on escorting him out before locking up. "Have a good night, Osin." "Where exactly am I supposed to go? A movie?"

She shrugged. "Not my concern."

He stood in the driveway and watched her car pull out. There was something in her cold attitude that was rather exciting. It seemed more like play fighting, a Beatrice and Benedick scenario. In fact, she probably didn't want him to leave at all. Osin went into the garage, got the spare key, and let himself back into the house.

Back in his armchair, he tried to read but had difficulty concentrating. Why would Rosanna want to make him jealous? As payback, or because she wanted to push him to make a decision about her. Financially, she didn't need to remarry—she lived okay. It couldn't be sex. She never went in that much for it, and now the fires must surely be wetted.

Could it be that she was still in love with him? Maybe she'd been waiting years in this little house for him to come back. With Rosanna it was hard to tell; she didn't have Merrill's emotional transparency. She was always very private, repressed even, squashing impulses before she was even fully aware of them. There was a time, during the marriage, when Osin used to force her to get angry just so he could see some passion in her. It always ended with her red-faced and straining, saying, "I don't know."

He must have fallen asleep in his chair; he woke up to the heavy slam of a car door, then another slam. The trunk? Osin peered out the window at the two shadowy figures coming up the walk. He should go to his room, but what if she brought the man up to the bedroom, thinking Osin was out. Had she seen his car? Only if she had gone into the garage. The key turned in the lock. She caught him mid-stride in the kitchen. "Osin!"

She was drunk; he could see that. Her lipstick looked smeared too, as if she'd just been kissing.

Behind her was a brown-haired man in a suit jacket that was too large. He couldn't have been over forty. The weedy mustache made him seem even younger, a weathered thirty-five. He looked like he had a civil service job, or maybe something janitorial.

"I apologize, George." Rosanna gestured dismissively in Osin's direction. "This is my tenant. He's usually up in his room at this hour."

"Osin Vachell, Rosanna's husband." He shook hands. "Good meeting you. Can I interest you in a scotch? She's got a twelve-year. It's not bad."

"No, thanks," George said, frowning.

"Ex-husband," Rosanna said. "We've been divorced for years." She was worrying her hands, which made Osin think she'd been caught out in a lie. Under different circumstances, he would have felt sorry for her.

They all stood around awkwardly for a minute, Osin still beaming his false, proprietary smile. "Let's *all* have a drink!"

"I should be getting home," George said.

"Nonsense. It's early yet, and you're a young man— the youngest in the room."

"I have a babysitter."

"A babysitter? You're not married are you?"

"No. I'm divorced."

"Full custody?"

"Osin!" Rosanna said, and then apologized to George again on his behalf.

He'd heard all he needed to. The guy had kids, probably ran out on his last wife, and besides that he was humorless and blamed everyone else for his own problems. Rosanna sure knew how to pick 'em. This was another thing he'd learned from the children and divorce book—the wife had a tendency to repeat the pattern of unhealthy relationships.

"Well, all right then," he said. "Drive safely."

Osin let Rosanna walk George to the door and do whatever last minute groping she wanted. When she came back in the room, he was still standing. "I'm sorry if that was awkward for you. I didn't think you'd bring him home so soon. It was only the first date."

"You have some nerve breaking into my house!"

"I didn't break in. You leave the key in open view."

"Osin, you're such an asshole. How about showing me a little respect?"

He waited for tears. None came. He felt the heat of the courtship dance again. She did look quite stunning in those clothes.

"Did it occur to you that maybe I was being protective?"

"You left me alone for twenty years. You're just territorial, like a dog is. It has nothing to do with me."

"Well, maybe things have changed. Maybe I do care now. Too much." He waited, but she didn't pick this up. "You must have known I'd come back in here."

"I'd hoped you'd be a better man than that."

"You didn't go out on the date just to make me jealous?"

She snorted. "I date a lot, you know. You're just lucky I wasn't with someone I liked." She pointed to the dining room. "I left that light on, and you turned it off. Saving electric?"

"If you knew I was here, why'd you bring him in!"

"To prove a point. I thought you'd rush upstairs. But it backfired because for some reason you're acting entitled to me tonight."

This statement made him uncomfortable. The drink had loosened her tongue, and the entire conversation seemed to be skittering around. Who knew what she was liable to say? "You should watch yourself. George is going to think you have loose morals."

"You know what I don't understand?" She went over to the liquor cabinet and opened it with a clumsy grab. "Here you have this young wife and you still talk like it's 1956."

"Hey. Easy, okay."

"It's almost like she had the reverse effect. She aged you." Rosanna took out the crème de menthe and poured herself a glass. "Want one?"

He shook his head, as she came by with the bottle. She kicked off her shoes and stretched her nylon legs out on the sofa. "Are you getting back together with her?" Her eyes narrowed aggressively at him.

"Hey, you're the one who encouraged it."

"Yes." She rubbed her temple—a sign she was feeling overtired. "But then take over negotiations from your own house. Not mine."

"Why do you always throw that in my face?"

"Because it's exceedingly bizarre that you just moved in here unannounced. I'm willing to let it go as a strange episode in my later life. Like the stray cat under the porch I was feeding all winter. But that doesn't mean I'm not watching you." She took a sip of her drink. "Your days here are numbered."

"Can we talk about this later? Maybe when you're not sauced?"

He expected a reaction, but she just stared back at him with her big, placid eyes.

"And for your information," Osin continued, "Merrill and I aren't making amends. Things are just as bad as they were when you were in charge."

"Okay," she lifted her hands, "onto another topic. We went to that fish place on San Pedro. The one that just opened up."

Osin was unfamiliar with her neighborhood. "I don't know it."

"George is an ethnographer. A rather brilliant man. He teaches at San Francisco State now."

Another brilliant man who most likely wasn't. Osin wondered if Rosanna remembered how much he detested academics. "I don't want to hear the details of the night. Let's talk about something else."

"He reminds me a little of Fritz Fitzen. Remember him?" Her hand swept the end table where a group of ceramic animals used to hold court. "Where's my turtle?"

Osin had been slowly transferring the living room knickknacks into a box in the attic. He shrugged. "Maybe Bernard pinched it. Listen, there's something I've been meaning to ask you. Have you ever dated the neighbor?"

"Which neighbor?"

"The fat one across the street. With the socks."

"Jim?" she said. "No. What gave you that idea?"

"He's always staring over here. Even from inside his house. He obviously doesn't understand the concept of backlighting at night."

"He probably doesn't like you nosing around. Especially when I'm out. He's head of the neighborhood watch."

"Your house is the only one he watches."

"Well he's been nothing but nice to me since he moved in." Rosanna slid over a coaster and put her drink down. "But you know who did try and pick me up?"

"No."

"Guess."

"I'm not guessing." He disliked her drunken confessing, but he was unwilling to go upstairs quite yet.

"Fritz. It was when you and I were still married, too."

"Fitzen?" Fritz's dart-shaped head suddenly came into focus. "When?"

"At that party we went to at the Ambassador, for his daughter's graduation."

Osin dimly remembered the place with its padded red walls, like the interior of a ship. Anger rose in him. "That skunk! With his faux French. I remember he used to say *enchanté* when he shook your hand."

Rosanna took a sip of her drink, smacking her lips. "After you and I separated, I let him take me on a date."

"What! How could you?"

"I was very confused then."

"So how far you'd go with him? You bring him home too?"

"Yup," she said.

"Rosanna! You didn't have sex with him, did you?"

She didn't answer right away, and Osin felt his chest go hollow.

"Don't look so glum," she said.

"I can't believe you did that. How many times?"

"Just once."

Osin tried to picture his angry, pageboy wife with Fitzen laboring on top. He came up with the smug Rosanna of now. "That prick. He looked liked he went to dirty movie houses and peep shows. You could tell by the way he walked. Like he was ashamed of something." He shook his head. "This whole time I just thought you had gone into therapy. Talking over what a schnook I was."

"Nope." She uncrossed her legs and stood up.

"He was a car salesman, for christsake! Well, at least now we're even. Although it's not much consolation."

"Even! For your affairs during our marriage! You've got to be kidding me." She shook her head. "No way."

"Why do you always have to be in the right? You're flawed, too."

"Maybe a little," she said. "But you have no ethics."

"I have ethics! How can you say that?"

She yawned. "I'm done with this conversation. I'm going to bed."

Passing by him, she suddenly bent down close to his face; he could feel the heat coming off her. "Next time you break into my house," she said, "I'm getting out the shotgun." She stood up and the dress' hem brushed against the exposed skin of his calf. A tremor ran through him. Not desire exactly, something more muted, a longing for contact.

She was already across the room. "Good night."

Osin watched her shifting, silky form go up the stairs.

The next afternoon Merrill called while Osin was sitting on the toilet, thinking about Fitzen. "Look," he told her, "I'm tiring of these games. I'm too old to be sneaking around."

"Who's sneaking around? We're just talking."

"This ambiguity." He sighed. "I'm thinking of putting through divorce proceedings." He was trying to get a rise out of her, but when he said the word "divorce," he realized that it sounded practical. It was what he should do.

There was an icy pause on her end. "You can't be serious."

"We aren't compatible. You're right. We fought a lot about money, ideas, different things."

She didn't disagree. "You really want a divorce?"

"I don't know. Let's meet and discuss it."

"When?"

"How about tomorrow night?"

"Saturday?" She hesitated. "I have plans."

"Then change them." It was the only time he could slip out without Rosanna noticing. "I don't want to put this off any more." He sighed. "It's too draining."

"Okay, okay. I can do it at seven. How about that place where I used to meet you for cocktails after work. Imbruglio? It was near the Embarcadero. It'll be nice to go there again."

"Yeah, sure, whatever." He heard Rosanna coming down the hall. "Seven's fine."

Saturday afternoon Osin and Richard had scheduled a trip to a lumberyard in the city, on Harrison. Richard had suggested it, but in the car he was cold and seemed hassled. Osin didn't talk much. After hanging up with Merrill, he realized he'd made a grave mistake scheduling this meeting. What if she actually was intending to leave Eric and come back to him? A couple of drinks and he would at least want to have sex with her. Rosanna seemed to know something was going on. She had been acting funny all morning.

At the yard Osin chose a high grade of mahogany that Richard, with the salesperson's help, talked him out of.

"For a tool bench, Dad? You've got to be out of your mind."

Osin liked the idea of giving Rosanna something more upscale than her life warranted. He settled on oak, which he could varnish.

Afterwards Osin was feeling nostalgic; he convinced Richard to walk with him up into the financial district. It was the lunch hour on a mild Friday afternoon. Men and women poured out of the buildings. "That used to be me," he said. "All dappered up in a suit. I passed that Wells Fargo Bank every day for years." Day after day. It was the consistent thread that ran through the middle of his life, tying up all its parts. Today, in the strong sunlight, those years seemed pointless, already replaced.

"I remember I came to visit you once at work," Richard said. "You took me out to lunch and called me your client."

Osin had a vague memory of his small son peering over the desk, dressed in pleated khakis and a dark tie. "Was this another one of those days when I force fed you?"

Richard didn't smile. "No, this was earlier. Before you left. I don't know how young I was, but I remember riding up in the copper elevator."

They crossed Market, scattering the pigeons that congregated near the gutter. Osin felt heat coming from the pavement and the heavy rush of traffic. The city never suited him, he decided, even though he'd spent the majority of his life there. He had always been much more of a nature man. "I always wanted to own a ranch," he said aloud, continuing the thought. "Maybe I should have."

"I'm glad you didn't," said Richard. "I can just imagine the amount of repair work that would need."

"I would have hired someone."

Richard shrugged his big, workman shoulders—a strange gesture for a man his age.

"You know I tried to give you money for a down payment on a house when you first married. Your mother wouldn't let me. She said you and Judy weren't ready to buy. I never should have listened to her. Think of the way property values have gone up."

"It wasn't mom's fault," Richard said. "I wouldn't accept the money."

"You knew about that?" At the time he was barely speaking to any of them. Richard was upset about a comment Osin had made about Judy, and he and Rosanna were on bad terms because he'd just moved in with Merrill. "Why did she lie to me about it?"

"I don't know. Maybe she didn't want your feelings to be hurt."

Osin had always found Rosanna's selflessness intimidating. But now that he felt himself to be a better person, or at least moving in that direction, it was something he could appreciate. This large-scale generosity was tough to nurture, although probably easier for Rosie. The particular ethical configuration of each person is different— she, on the other hand, had a problem saying no, which was very easy for him.

So they were both faulty, although he was admittedly worse. There was this clandestine meeting with Merrill, for one; the anticipation of it, on the fringes of his consciousness, changed the day. He was hyperaware of the street corner, the edges of the building, Richard's profile in the sun. An exhilarating and shameful secret he was keeping, during this excursion that was supposed to bond them together.

"I have to check on a rug that Judy ordered at Nordstrom," Richard said.

Osin spotted a sunny outdoor table. "I'll wait for you over there."

Richard shrugged again. He seemed indifferent to Osin's company. Why was Ritchie here at all? Maybe, like Osin, he felt some lingering responsibility. Although, it was probably because Rosanna, or even Osin's own treacherously aged body, was reminding Richard of his father's mortality. Better to make amends now before the old man kicks off.

Walking to his table, he passed a flower stall where Merrill was standing, holding a bouquet of roses. For a split second Osin didn't recognize her. When he did, he made a surprised gurgle.

The rose stems leaked water onto the pavement. "Osin! Did you follow me?"

He was offended. "No! I wasn't even thinking about you. I'm here with Richard."

"Richard! Since when do you pal around with him?"

Osin looked around quickly. His son was nowhere in sight. "We're working things out. He has some legitimate gripes from the divorce. But I've been reading up—"

"Listen, I'm having some trouble getting out of my plans tonight. Eric's acting suspicious."

"I didn't realize you were doing this on the sly."

"Are you crazy? Do you think I'm going to tell him? I'm supposed to meet him back by the car in a couple of minutes."

"He's here?" Osin started to get edgy. "I can't discuss this right now, either. Richard's going to be out any minute."

"Maybe if I tell Eric I'm going out with Laurel," Merrill said. "That she's having a crisis, maybe something with her husband."

There was something in Merrill's expression that was very familiar. Osin got a sinking feeling. "Right before you moved out, you kept needing to go to counsel Lauren. Don't tell me you were seeing Eric then?"

She stared at him. With her free hand, she pushed the hair back from her forehead. She could have been one of a million career women buying flowers on a weekend afternoon, dressed in a pink blouse he didn't recognize.

"Oh, Merrill. Honestly, I don't have the energy for this again."

"It's just a drink. I'm not promising anything."

"No, you were right. It's a bad idea. Let's just forget it." Osin looked towards the department store entrance. No Richard. His gaze shifted to the foreground where a bald man had stopped in the middle of the sidewalk and was giving him a white-hot stare. He had a froggy little mouth, the fat upper lip hanging over the lower. "Is that Eric?"

"What?" Merrill turned.

Eric was striding over to them. His hair had thinned on top; it seemed to be falling out from stress, like the feathers from a nervous parrot. Osin looked down at Eric's feet. No sneakers. He had on black loafers.

"What do you think you're doing?" Eric shouted.

Osin took a half step backwards, so that he almost trod on Merrill's shoe. "I'm just talking to her."

"Yeah, right. Okay. Good. Let's settle this."

Merrill wedged herself in between them; she tried to get a hold of Eric's shoulder, but he ducked out of her grasp.

"Come on, old man," Eric said, stepping closer to Osin. "You had the balls to prank call us in the middle of the night."

Osin's throat went dry. A direct threat usually had that effect. He coughed. And then, from the corner of his vision, he saw Richard approaching. Osin turned his back, hoping Richard would keep on walking.

"Dad? What's going on here?"

Eric said, "He's harassing my girlfriend, the pervert." He got up close to Osin. "You know I never liked you, you son of a bitch."

"It's okay," Merrill said to no one in particular. Again, she grabbed Eric's shoulder. "Stop. We're leaving."

Richard looked confused, and Osin realized he probably thought there was yet another girl Osin had gotten in trouble with. "That's Merrill," Osin said, pointing to her. "Remember Merrill?"

Eric said, "He's been sneaking around the house in the middle of the night. Watching us through the windows like some dirty fucking pervert!"

"I didn't go to look in the windows," Osin said, lamely. Jesus, what would his son think? He turned to Richard. "I didn't see anything. And it was only once. To drop off a letter."

He expected Richard to start grilling him, but instead his son had turned to Eric. "She's still his wife. If they want to talk, that's their business."

"I don't want to talk to her!" Osin blurted, ashamed of himself.

"Thanks a lot," she said. He had hurt her. He could see it.

Eric kept trying to get into Osin's face. "You better not harass us again."

"Seriously, I don't have the stomach for this," Osin said. "Richard, let's go."

Richard was heated up. He seemed to have grown in size, so he towered over all of them. "You bother my father again, you so much as look at him, and you'll have to go through me." He grabbed Osin by the elbow, as if he were an old lady, and steered him into the street.

"Well that was humiliating," Osin said, as they approached the car. Being around his own son like a damsel in distress. But he was also perversely proud, or grateful for Richard. Was this what women walked around feeling like? "That Eric's a lunatic. No wonder Merrill wants to get away from him. I'm surprised you stuck up for me back there. I would have thought you wanted Eric to clobber me."

Richard's expression made it clear he held Osin responsible for the incident. "You shouldn't have been harassing her."

"I wasn't. Ask your mother. The letter was her idea." When Richard frowned, Osin said, "Your mother's not a pushover, you know. She has her own opinions. Anyway, I've asked Merrill for a divorce. We're through."

"Another divorce."

"What? Would you prefer I stayed with her?" Osin hunched in his seat. "You know for all your bad childhood memories, you don't seem that psychically damaged. You have a happy marriage. Love notes and all that."

Richard's face was unreadable. "I don't know who told you that."

"Your mother. Who else?"

"Well, it's not all wonderful."

Was this his fault too? "Everyone is going to have a little trouble now and again." He sounded like he was channeling Rosanna. He hesitated—what the hell. "Judy's a good woman. You got a great kid." It occurred to Osin that he wasn't in the best position to be dispensing marital wisdom, but Richard nodded.

He went on, "Listen, I would appreciate it if you didn't mention this run-in to your mother. She gets a little crazy when Merrill comes up in conversation."

With obvious emotion, Richard said, "This is the last lie I'm going to keep for you."

"On second thought don't. It's okay. I had no right to ask something like that. It's just the entire situation was humiliating."

"Well, I wouldn't lose any sleep over it. That guy's a loser. She already seems like she regrets going with him."

Richard turned up the radio, an old rock-and-roll song, *Led Zeppelin*, maybe, that Osin remembered drifting from his teenage son's room. They listened together, their windows rolled down, the breeze ruffling some papers in the backseat. Osin rested his arm on the door. Rosanna would be pleased with this. He hoped she was home, so he could tell her. But as they pulled in the driveway, he saw everyone was there—Judy, Bernard, Rosanna. They were standing on the porch in an accusatory little group.

Judy approached the car, angrily, pulling Bernard behind. As Richard got out, she said, "Bernard, tell your father what you just told me."

"About what?"

"About the house with the lady."

What the hell were they talking about? Rosanna hung in the background, her forehead wrinkled in concern.

"Oh. There was a lady there. She was nice, sort of nice. And grampy was there, and there were some balloons. There were stairs that go in a circle that make you dizzy. I got dizzy. But I want to wear the shirt and Mommy can't find it. I want to wear it today!"

"What shirt?" Richard asked Judy. Osin cringed.

"It seems your father—" Judy pointed at Osin— "took Bernard to his ex-wife's house when he said he was going to the aquarium."

"Dad! How could you take my son to Eric's house?" Richard looked disappointed, confused, betrayed. It was the most vulnerable look he'd seen on his son's face in years.

"No! We didn't go to Eric's! We stopped at an open house in Noe Valley. Eric wasn't even there. We were there for a very short time, it was literally a stop-in. This was so long ago, before I knew the man was aggressive. And then we did go to the aquarium. We saw the sharks." He was drowning, he knew he was. But how could he explain that all this, the meeting with Merrill, the secret phone calls, the adultery, all of it belonged to a past life that was as distant and insubstantial as the one he had experienced walking past his office building.

Bernard was tugging on Judy's sweater. "We saw sharks! They breathe through their neck. With gills. And I put my hand in the water. Don't be mad at Grampy."

"That was still very foolish, Osin," Rosanna said quietly.

Judy said, "You used my son to get your ex-wife back?"

Osin, who in the old days would have mounted a defense, said, "I'm sorry. It's inexcusable." He didn't dare look at Richard.

"And what's this about the shirt? Was it *her* shirt you made him wear?"

"No, no. It was just a shirt that said 'I forgive you'. To Merrill."

"Jesus Christ," Judy said.

They were still standing in the driveway. Why was it that the most awful scenes of Osin's life all took place here?

The wind kicked up, blowing Judy's hair up in all directions. He was reminded of a spectre rising from the depths of hell. Of all the people standing here that he'd wronged, this one, who he'd done nothing to, would make him pay.

Judy spoke with what was supposed to be restraint, but sounded more like hysteria. "You're not to see Bernard ever again. Never again, do you hear me? And we want you out of this house. Out!"

Osin felt the blood go into his face. It was a sentence you'd give a murderer. Was it possible that he'd never been forgiven by any of them? That the day he'd set foot in Rosanna's house, he'd come back to stand trial and just hadn't known?

"Okay," he said. "I understand."

"Judy," Richard took her stony arm, "I know you're upset, but you're being harsh. This is Bernard's grandfather. He adores him. Bernard was never in any real danger."

"We just saw Merrill downtown," Osin said. "It's over. I'm through with her," he told Rosanna.

"Why are you telling me this?" she said.

"Because I know you care about it more than you let on. We ran into Merrill on the street and Richard really came through. He handled an embarrassing situation with a lot of diplomacy. I was ashamed at first that he saw me—" the gushing, he should really stop himself. His son—how had he raised someone better than himself? Judy was staring at him, angry, defeated, and bewildered. "Listen, Judy, I don't have to see the boy until you feel more comfortable about the situation. It was a dumb thing I did and I'm sorry. But I do love the kid, and I want to see him grow up."

"He does stupid things, but he's not malicious," Rosanna said.

"It was very stupid," Osin said. "Thoughtless."

Judy turned to Richard, "I want to go home now."

"I should go too," Osin said with relief.

Rosanna looked surprised. "I'll call you," he told her, as he got into his car. He followed Richard's truck with his family packed inside, to where the road split off to the highway.

V

That fall Judy went back to school. In the network of scheduling that Osin still wasn't consulted on, Bernard was spending the weekdays at Rosanna's. He showed up at the door already weary, as if he were punching the clock. Behind him he dragged along his luggage and a satchel of Japanese plastic dolls, talking plush things, and a few of the old standards—Exxon trucks and Legos. The sack sat unopened during the visit, although Bernard would pat it over regularly to see that nothing had gone missing. It seemed to stress him. "Don't bother bringing the toys next time," Osin told Judy. "He prefers to play with Rosanna's ceramics."

Bernard usually got his second wind at around ten-thirty. Then he was full of ideas, large-scale plans, and chatter. He got down to work on something after lunch. He was a bright kid—the over-affection was a bit of ruse. He actually seemed to prefer time alone.

From across the dining room table, Osin said, "You look like you're enjoying yourself." Bernard was frowning over an old coloring book that Rosanna had dug up. The light spread across his blond head. Osin went on, "You'll want to keep a hold of those critical faculties, you know. This place can suck you in."

Osin was reviewing the boat research he'd lifted off the Internet. He was wearing Rosanna's reading glasses because he couldn't find his own. She was right—this was a huge project; he was going to have to clear out the rest of the garage and maybe part of the patio. As it was, Richard had taken over operations on the tool bench, which was rapidly becoming a potting bench. Rosanna kept resting her trowels on the half finished boards. Osin cross-referenced the confused diagram with the one in his boat-building manual. When were you supposed to attach the transom knees?

He called out to Rosanna, "The hardest part is going to be cutting the mold panels. You have to get them just right. And for your information, you don't have to cure the wood. It bends because it's thin plywood."

He was going to need Richard's help on installing the gunnels. Probably even earlier than that. The kid knew his material, and he was a born pedagogue. He'd get up beside you while you were doing something as simple as tacking in a nail and point out how it should be angled. The right subject and he could kill you with talk. Who would have thought?

Osin looked at the picture of the boat builder, who was squatly gripping the oars of his finished creation. He was in the middle of a pond somewhere in the Northeast. "Hey, listen to this guy. He said he built his in thirty-eight man hours."

Bernard put one finger on the laminated book cover. It left a sticky crescent. "Is that your boat?"

Osin peered at him from over the glasses. "How did you know about that?"

Bernard gave a big sigh. "Daddy said. He said..." Osin waited for more, but the kid went back to crayoning.

Osin called out to Rosanna, "So Richard talks about me when I'm not around."

"He may even be saying good things." She had moved into the living room; it sounded as if she was sitting in the tatty armchair by the door.

Osin leaned over and whispered to Bernard, "What's he say about me?"

"Who?"

"Osin!" Rosanna appeared in the doorway. "Stop that."

"I thought you'd be pleased I was showing an interest in Richard." He turned to Bernard. "We can finish this later when the old lady ain't around."

"Come on," she said to Bernard, dropping a hand on his head. Her delicate long fingers smoothed his hair. Osin had a stirring memory of the way that felt, the fingertips running his scalp from behind the earlobes to his crown.

"It's time for your nap," she told Bernard. Resigned, the boy shut his book and went with her into the living room.

Osin tried to concentrate on the instructions for cutting a sculling notch. But instead he listened to Rosanna reading a story about bears that travel through the woods to attend a family picnic. A breeze came in from the windows. "And then what happened, if they had no food?" Bernard said, but his voice was already trailing off. Osin remembered when Richard was a baby they used to let him sleep in the bed between them, even though all the books said not to. Back then Rosanna had long hair she would sometimes tie back with a red and pink scarf. There was something very sexy about her in that scarf. Whenever he'd find it laying around the house, dropped over the arm of a chair, or hung over the towel rack, he'd feel a rush, as if he'd caught her naked.

Osin hoisted himself up from the table and went into the other room. Bernard lay asleep on his back, a blue blanket across his chest; his cheeks were flushed. Rosanna was by the fireplace, bent over her sewing basket. Osin came up behind her, slipping his hand down the top of her blouse and around one breast.

"Oh," she said in a surprised voice.

"How about we go upstairs." To his own ears, his voice sounded husky.

She turned around, and he saw an ironic flickering in her face. "What are you doing?"

Osin was taken aback. "You don't remember?"

"Remembering isn't the problem."

His hand was still wedged in her shirt. "Do you want me to stop?" He bent in and kissed her a little awkwardly, her mouth seemed oddly empty. He pictured it as dark and winding, like a vacant burrow. But then they established a rhythm, as in the old days. Her tongue, when she used it, was flat and warm. He thought briefly of Merrill's—cool and probing as an instrument. She had stopped calling him, and he felt, finally, that he could relax.

When he pulled away, he saw Rosanna's face had softened. Her misty eyes refocused on his chin. Feeling a stab of misgiving, he took her hand and led her towards the stairs.

At the top landing, he pulled her into his room. Her bedroom, their marital bed, would be too fraught. She must have been through here earlier because the shade was up, and the sun came in on his old desk. The bed-covers were rumpled, as if the sexual act had already taken place. Even now, things were a little iffy below the belt. Rosanna took his pajama bottoms, where they lay splay-legged across the pillow, and folded them onto the chair. "This will be strange," she said.

Osin kissed her again, near the ear. Her hair smelled powdery, like the upstairs bathroom. He unbuttoned the blouse, wishing for a moment that it had a Peter Pan collar. They stood on the rug, facing each other. He kissed her shoulder. Walking around the house, he'd always thought Rosanna smelled vaguely of dryer sheets, but up close this scent was a muskier, more sour bodily one. It shocked him to think that he couldn't really remember Merrill's scent. But perhaps the sense of smell is fickle. He'd be rooting through the house one day, years from now, and the smell would knock him over. The house— he really should check on that.

Unhooking Rosanna's bra, he was surprised to see the port wine stain underneath her armpit. "I'd forgotten you had this," he said. "The European continent." He kissed it. The skin tasted salty.

"You used to always do that," she said.

They collapsed in a heated tangle onto the bed. She reached down to unzip him, and he shifted to accommodate her fingers, which were surprisingly practiced. But still he sensed a weakening energy in his pants, substantiated when he looked down. She massaged the tired member, trying to pump some life into it. He called up his best fantasy images—three tall blonds in a steam room, then in a sauna, then at a massage parlor.

He slid his hand inside her underwear. There was so much hair there. He parted it with his fingers, looking for the slick parts. Perhaps the moisture just hadn't spread yet. He touched the lips. Nothing. She was still squeezing him, although the rhythm had slowed. He flattened his hand. They lay there, on their backs, exhausted.

"Well, I guess that's not going to work," Rosanna said finally, sliding her hand out of the boxer shorts. She stared up at the ceiling. One of her breasts lolled to the side, its dark nipple grazing his arm.

After a moment Osin said, "Sorry."

"Wrong thing to apologize for. But you did start it."

"You weren't exactly hot and heavy, either."

"This isn't a competition. And you caught me off guard. I was getting ready to hem a pair of pants."

Osin laughed, but Rosanna, her face adverted, said, "I guess I'm not the hot ticket Merrill is."

Osin was surprised that she still had the vanity to get offended. "No. That's not it. Even with Merrill I used to take the pills. They're back at the house."

"What pills?" He felt her weight shift in his arms. "Viagra?"

He nodded. He was beyond the point of defending himself about the medicine. "It was Merrill's idea. Little did I know I'd become hooked."

"I don't think it's addictive. Does it work?"

He nodded.

"Well, that's news to me. I thought it was just a big marketing scam."

"Maybe we just rushed at this too early," he said.

"What, you mean sex? We don't know each other well enough?"

"Don't laugh at me," he said. "I'm about to say something profound. We're not used to each other in the sexual context. Maybe after a certain amount of time, the clock resets, and we have to re-learn our relationship."

She rolled over to face him. "Are you reading another self-help book?"

"It was an article," he confessed. "In *Modern Maturity*."

"You really like that magazine. You bring it from the mailbox to your bedroom before I get a chance to look at it."

The bed springs squeaked as he shifted his weight. "Why did you let me stay here? Was it because you felt sorry for me, or because you thought I was going to harm myself, maybe die, and then it would be on your conscience the rest of your life."

"I took you in because I loved you."

What a comforting word "love" was. How easy it was for her to fend off that suffocating darkness. What would have happened if she had turned him away when he first arrived? But he had known she wouldn't. That's why he drove here.

She lay her head back down on his chest. He watched it rise and fall with his breath. "You know, this room is pretty nice. I never come in here anymore."

"Yeah," Osin agreed. "I used to like working in here during the afternoons. Because of the southern exposure." Lying with her changed the dimensions of the room, jogged his memory back to when he used to do his taxes, staring out at the rustling leaves of the oak tree.

"Think I should paint?" Rosanna asked.

Osin never noticed, but the walls were cracking along the corners. "I'll do it. It's my room."

"Not exactly," she said.

"I'm thinking of selling my house," he said. "It's too big for me alone, anyway."

"You put the divorce papers through with Merrill?"

"Yes," he said. "She didn't put up much of a fight, either, although the alimony will probably be steep." He put one hand on the top of Rosanna's head, paternally. "So, how would you like it if I moved in here?"

She laughed. "No way."

"Why not? We get along great as housemates."

"No, we don't," she said.

The light had moved to the floor, where it lay in triangles. He heard the ticking of the hallway clock, and a lawnmower start up in the distance; then he heard Rosanna's breath easing off into sleep. Wrapped around him, her body felt soft and flexible. Twisting slightly, he looked down at her. She had beautiful eyes when closed; they were perfect semicircles. He tried to sleep, too, but the blueprints for the boat were printed on the inside of his lids. He pictured the smooth dark wood, the sturdy seat, himself drifting out on the flat water, casting with his fishing rod. He thought backwards to the work, the sanding and fitting and staining, the sawhorses in a narrow garage. There was so much to do. The blanket had gotten bunched around his hip, and he freed it, pulling it over Rosanna's shoulders. Quietly, he got out of bed and went downstairs, where his plans were waiting for him.

All of my thanks to the following people: my parents and Graham for their support and encouragement; my BU writing group, especially Jen Stroup, Jacob Drew, Alex Ortolani, and David Khoury for their critical suggestions. I have greatly benefited from three gifted writers and teachers, Leslie Epstein, Marshall Klimasewiski, and Ha Jin, to whom this book is particularly indebted. Many thanks, as well, to my excellent editors at Low Fidelity, Tobin and Brad; Aimee Bender; Kara Decas; and to Mariève Rugo for all of her literary insight.

Also Available from Low Fidelity Press

Rabbit Punches
Stories by Jason Ockert

Riotously funny, beautifully written, and charged with emotional intelligence, this well-crafted debut investigates the world from the fringe through characters who stray so far from convention they seem to inhabit another universe.
ISBN 0-9723363-5-4

Next Door Lived a Girl
by Stefan Kiesbye

Winner of the Low Fidelity's 2004 Novella Award, Stefan Kiesbye's powerful debut is an investigation into the feral adolescent world of post-war Germany. Peter Ho Davies calls it, "(A) dark, distinctive vision of humanity, composed with such narrative skill and verve as to render the bleakness bracing, the grimness utterly gripping."
ISBN 0-9723363-2-X

On the Way to My Father's Funeral: New and Selected Stories
by Jonathan Baumbach

Thirteen new stories and Baumbach's selected together in a single collection for the first time. Baumbach's fiction has appeared in *Transgressions: The Iowa Anthology of Innovative Fiction*, *The Best American Short Stories*, and *The O. Henry Prize Stories*.
ISBN 0-9723363-3-8

The Week You Weren't Here
by Charles Blackstone

The Week You Weren't Here is a poignant and wry portrait of a young writer closing in on the last of his undergraduate days. Matthew Roberson calls it, "A smart, fun book that takes a fascinating look at the minutiae that complicate our (love) lives."
ISBN 0-9723363-4-6

Trouble with the Machine
Poems by Christopher Kennedy

In his newest collection of prose poems, *Trouble with the Machine*, Christopher Kennedy again takes us on a tour of his brilliantly odd-ball world. Kennedy's poetry is fiercely comic, deliciously irreverent, and a welcome oasis in the dry landscape of modern poetry.
ISBN 0-9723363-1-1

Available online at www.lofipress.com